T0162868

SIRENS' SONG

Book One of the Wolves of Albany

By Jerrard E Weigler

authorHOUSE®

AuthorHouse™
1663 Liberty Drive
Bloomington, IN 47403
www.authorhouse.com
Phone: 1-800-839-8640

First published by AuthorHouse 3/21/2011

ISBN: 978-1-4567-4430-4 (sc)
ISBN: 978-1-4567-4431-1 (dj)
ISBN: 978-1-4567-4432-8 (e)

Library of Congress Control Number: 2011902375

Printed in the United States of America

TABLE OF CONTENTS

1: Don't Cry Wolf

I t was a Saturday night in the small town of Albany, Illinois. Everything was normal here. Everyone knew one another and lived in a calm peaceful environment. Or at least as peaceful as any other small town in America would be on a Saturday.

Around three o'clock am a call came in to the police station about a party in progress that was getting a bit too rowdy. The dispatch worker, a woman by the name of Alexis, assumed that the disturbance was just a bunch of teenagers that had a bit too much to drink. She put the call out to the have one of the squad cars run by to check on the situation.

"Sure thing Alexis, I'm about three blocks from there right now," responded Sgt. Shawn Darvis. "Just have Rudi meet me there. I may need back up. Over."

"Will do," Alexis replied "Over and out."

Sgt. Darvis has always kept in fairly good shape. He never seemed to be able to lose his spare tire, but he wore it well. Even with the fact that he started losing his dark brown hair that he always kept cut short and styled in his early twenties, he still retained confidence in his looks; though, he never got too cocky about the fact that he was handsome.

When Darvis pulled up to the house that was said to be causing the disturbance, he heard instantly why the call was made. He could hear a radio blaring as well as yelling. He even thought it sounded as though there may be a fight breaking out in the back. And so he decided that waiting till Officer Rudi Demko arrived would probably be a good idea.

After waiting about five minutes, Rudi finally turned the corner to back-up Shawn. Rudi, the rookie of the small group of cops in Albany, had a kid in a candy store grin spread across his face when he hopped out of his squad car.

Rudi was a short young man that was only twenty-two. He did not seem bothered by the fact that he was the youngest officer on the police force in Albany. It was the fact that he was almost a head shorter than the rest of his co-workers that annoyed him. Standing only five feet five inches was sure to give any man a complex that was working in an authoritative position. Even though he was short, he was cocky and sure of himself in a way that raked on others around him. He was naturally tan and had a well developed muscular build form too much time in the gym during college. His dark hair and hazel eyes only added to the fact that he really was a good looking young man. However, he only had eyes for one woman, Alexis. He would give the world for the wavy haired blonde dispatch worker.

"Sarge, why haven't you gone in there and start crackin' skulls yet? You aren't afraid of a group of kids are ya?" Rudi, as always, was making a joke of the job.

'This was why he wouldn't make it on the force anywhere else,' thought Darvis. "Of course I'm not afraid of some kids. However, I do follow procedure. Something you need to learn to do if you ever want to get a promotion," Darvis spat angrily. He liked Rudi, really he did, he just would rather not have him working his shift. "Plus, we don't even know if the people causing the disturbance are kids back. Assuming stuff like that can get you killed in any other community. Just stay behind me and watch my back. And keep your damn mouth shut!"

"YES SIR!" Rudi barked back in his usual mocking tone. Darvis made a mental note to have him washing squad cars for the next month.

They made their way slowly and silently to the back yard where the commotion appeared to be coming from. When they got to where they could see what was going on in the back, they both froze. They could see a small group of people in their mid to late twenties. All of whom, the men and the women, were very muscular in build. And none of them were wearing socks; let alone any other article of clothing. And they all appeared to have blood smeared on them. Yet, no one seemed to be injured in any way.

Darvis started to get a bad feeling about what was going on. A part of his brain was screaming at him to run, but he couldn't do that when he had a job to do. Guess the badge over rules logic and reason. "Who's in charge here," Darvis asked, speaking loudly to be heard over the stereo and talking.

A tall brooding man with short dirty-blonde hair stepped forward from the crowd. He had an air to himself that commanded he be listened to and obeyed. Darvis knew instantly that he was the guy he had just called out, and wished he hadn't. Though he wasn't much bigger than the other guys around him, he had a power that seemed to radiate from him. Darvis' skin crawled when the man met his glare with one of his own.

"I was wondering when the bacon would show. I would be in charge here. The names Rowland," the big man stated. "Were we being too loud? We will try to keep it down."

While talking, the man kept getting closer. "Hold it there, sir," Darvis commanded. The man was putting him on edge; however, he wasn't entirely sure why. Something about him made the hair on the back of Darvis' neck stand on end. He placed his hand on his taser to comfort himself. Finally the man paused.

"You really don't want to do that." Rowland warned, seeing Darvis reaching for his taser. "we out number you. Even with your back-up that is lurking around the corner you couldn't take us all on. Plus, you wouldn't be able to hit me with that little stunner of yours. And if you did, you would regret it almost instantaneously."

"I assure you sir, I am a very good shot. And a damn quick draw," Darvis said, starting to get pissed. Anger helped him put on a brave face.

"I wasn't saying that your aim wouldn't be accurate. Rather that I would dodge it." And before Darvis could even blink, Rowland was behind him. Terror brought forth panic when Darvis glanced over his shoulder and looked into Rowland's once dark blue eyes. His eyes had turned an ice blue iridescent color that is never found in humans. "Plus, it wouldn't work on us. Though it would piss us off, and you don't want that. Yes, monsters do exist! And I suggest that you leave if you can't control your fear. I have restraint, but some of my new recruits don't. We will keep it down. Just don't come back out here tonight. I don't want to have to…"

Before he finished the last statement, his head snapped around as he swore. Darvis could see the barbs of a taser sticking out of Rowland's back. He knew then that Rudi had lost his cool and that they both were now in danger. But before he could attempt to calm Rowland, he already had Rudi pinned to the ground. He just stood there in shock as the man that was known as Rowland seemed to be changing in front of his eyes. His back rippled and his hands were turning to claws. Then, his teeth began to grow longer and sharper.

Darvis still hadn't collected himself when he heard shots being fired and a man yell. "Let him go Rowland! Now! Unless you want the next shot to be at your head! And you know I always use silver ammo incase you snapped someday." Darvis knew the voice before he saw the man. He was the Captain of the police department in Albany. His name was Jeff Stilwell.

Jeff was the youngest Captain that the town of Albany had ever had. At only thirty one, he planned to hold his position for some time. He still looked like a man in his mid twenties. Good genetics can have that effect on people. His light brown hair had started to become streaked with gray, which was the only indicator of his real age. He kept in shape by jogging every day and going to the gym any chance he got. Jeff was known and loved by everyone in the community. He was caring and always went out of his way to help, even on his days off.

Head buzzing from the events that were transpiring, Darvis watched as Rowland sank the claws that now had replaced the man's fingernails in to the rookie's neck. Blood started flowing as Rowland glared at Jeff. "He attacked me in front of my pack. That cannot go unpunished. You know that because I broke skin, even with only a partial transformation, he will become one of us. Then I can get my revenge." And Rowland stood and threw Rudi's body in one fluid movement that was just a blur. Rudi's body landed, limp in front of Jeff. Darvis ran to the boy's side to check on him. He was barely breathing, and the bleeding wasn't showing any signs that it was slowing.

Darvis took his shirt off to put pressure on the puncture holes in the kid's neck. Before he could, Jeff grabbed him. "We gotta get the hell outta here Shawn. The smell of blood will get them riled up and I only have enough ammo left to fend off a few of them. Let's get Rudi into the car," Jeff ordered. Darvis did what he was told and grabbed Rudi under the arm and hefted him toward the car.

By the time Jeff and Shawn had gotten Rudi into the back seat, the shirt around his neck had already become drenched in his blood. Shawn looked on with worry etched plainly on his face at the pale form of his co-worker as he gradually became more and more pale.

Finally pulling his gaze from the fallen officer, he asked; "Do you think he'll pull through?"

Jeff turned from the horrific scene in the back of his car with haunted eyes. "I know he'll pull through. Rowland made sure of that when he infected him. He will be nearly healed before we even get him to the ER."

"Sir, I don't understand. How can any of this be possible? And infected? Infected with what?"

"Not so long ago I would have wondered the same thing. Get in the car and I will fill you in on what little I know."

Without saying another word, Jeff turned and walked around to the driver's side door. He glanced at Darvis quickly, and then got in the car behind the wheel.

Darvis, still in shock, got in the passenger side and waited quietly as his Captain prepared to tell him what the hell was going in the sleepy little town of Albany.

"It all started when I met Rowland about around eleven months ago." Jeff began.

2: ROWLAND

"owland first moved back to town about a year ago. He was just a normal, almost nerdy young man. He was of average height and slightly overweight. At the time when he first came to Albany, he wore glasses. In fact, he couldn't see more than a few feet in front of himself without them. He had the same dirty blonde hair that you seen on him earlier. Only he was losing his hair back when we met. Having almost no hair left on top didn't seem to damper his confidence though. Obviously the balding didn't stick.

"He was a computer programmer fresh out of college and wanting to start up a little business in Albany. I bumped in to him at the bank and we became friends instantly.

"Everything was normal as could be, until a little over four months ago when Rowland and I decided to go on a hunting trip down in Calhoun County.

"The trip started ok. We went fishing the first day and planned to try for a deer the next day. When we entered the woods before the sun came up that morning, everything was freakishly quiet. But Rowland refused to turn back when I told him that I had a bad feeling. I felt like something terrible was about to happen if we didn't turn back right away.

"'Quit worrying old man,' Rowland had said. 'Nothing's going to happen. There isn't any big bad wolf in this neck of the woods out to get ya. Maybe a rabid raccoon might decide to bite you.'

"He laughed his ass off at his own joking. I didn't laugh myself, but I did start feeling silly.

"That's when I heard a noise behind us."

Darvis was staring at Jeff dumbfounded. Jeff had such a haunted look in his eyes. Jeff's eyes, which were a brilliant shade of green, usually

7

held such life and good humor. But now they looked hallow and empty of anything as he reluctantly relived the memory. The man in the driver's seat, in fact, did not seem much like the Jeff Stilwell that everyone in the community loved so much. He appeared to have aged instantly. The man went from being barely thirty to looking like he was pushing forty in front of Darvis' very eyes.

"It started as a rustling behind some bushes," Jeff continued. "Then, while peering into the spot where I had heard the noise, I saw a pair of glowing, yellow eyes. I couldn't figure out what it was.

"I shot once in the direction of the eyes to try and scare whatever it was away. However, all I did was pissed the fucking thing off.

"It growled and bolted at us from its hiding place so fast that I couldn't react.

"Rowland reacted with reflexes I wouldn't have thought a nerdy, slightly overweight man could possibly have. He shoved me out of the way. As I fell to the ground, the beast slammed into Rowland and they went tumbling out of sight. I remember seeing what appeared to be a giant wolf that was impossibly fast sink its teeth into Rowland's right arm as they rolled away.

"The world started to go dark and I felt something warm and liquid running down my face before I blacked out.

"When I came to I was alone and the sun was already high in the sky. I got slowly to my feet, fighting off waves of nausea. I couldn't see Rowland or the beast anywhere. I searched the area for more than an hour without seeing either of them. The strangest thing was that there didn't appear to be a sign of a struggle. Not even a blood trail.

"I went back to the cabin to look at my own injuries and to eat before heading back out to search some more. After eating a can of beef stew, I put on my boots and coat then headed for the door. That's when the door opened.

"Rowland came in with blood stained clothes that had been torn to shreds. I looked at him and couldn't believe what my eyes knew to be true. His injury that should have required many stitches was already covered in pink, new skin.

"He looked to be in better health then he had before the attack. I could have sworn that his muscle mass seemed to have increased in the few hours that had transpired since the attack. Besides the clothes being ruined, he was alright.

"'Man, Jeff, you look like you've seen a ghost or something,' Rowland said with a shit eating grin spread across his face. 'You don't look so good. What the hell happened to your head? Better yet, what happened this morning in general? The last thing I remember was you having a strange feeling, and then I woke up in the woods alone.'"

Darvis couldn't believe what he was hearing. It didn't make sense at all. How could a guy survive an attack like that? And, better yet, how could he be the same man he had seen not fifteen minutes earlier?

He sat patiently during Jeff's pause in the story. He dared to glance in the backseat even though he was afraid that Rudi may already be dead. But he appeared to be breathing more evenly and some of the color was returning to his face. How could that be possible?

Jeff cleared his throat to get Darvis' attention; and continued with his horrific story. "We didn't stick around the cabin much longer after I filled Rowland in on what little I remembered from that horrible morning.

"We headed back home that afternoon and didn't talk about what happened that day since.

"Rowland started going through a lot of strange changes in the month that followed. He grew stronger and faster. He craved meat all the time and barely cooked it which was strange because he was always a 'well done' kind of guy. His eye sight got better almost instantly. At first I thought contacts till he told me about the things that were going on with his body. His other senses got heightened as well.

"He and I exchanged witty banter about how he was becoming a superhero. If only we had known the truth. It isn't that he had become a bad guy or anything. In fact, he did kinda become a hero.

"It wasn't till he and I were out the night of the full moon that we learned what was really going on. That was when he changed into a werewolf for the first time. The transformation was terribly painful for him to go through at first. All of his bones breaking and reshaping to become just like the beast that had attacked him. The only differences were that Rowland's eyes had become an icy blue that bordered on white. And his coat was completely white, except the black tip on his tail.

"I wasn't even afraid of him after the change was complete. We later found out that he was different among his kind. During the first full moon of anyone's transformation the person changing would lose all sense of their humanity; becoming completely primal. But Rowland didn't have any of the problems with control that all those who have joined his pack seemed to have had. He was as gentle as a well trained dog.

"Hell, I played fetch with him.

"I have never seen him lose control like he had tonight. All the members of his pack were changed by him, with the exception of his second in command, Brian Roberts; but only after they convinced him to change them because it would save each of them from their own untimely deaths. Rudi will be the first he changed without consent. Rowland is going to feel terrible about this."

"Sir, how could that thing feel terrible about doing what he did? He seemed like he enjoyed making Rudi nearly bleed to death," Darvis inquired of his Captain.

The squad car came to a halt at a red light in the middle of town. Jeff turned to Darvis with a steely glare that made Darvis cringe under the weight of that stare. "Rowland is one of the best guys I have ever had the privilege of meeting," Jeff spat. "He has done more for our community than anyone on the force will do in a life time. We sleep safe at night because he and his pack are keeping the bad things away. It wasn't like he asked to be infected with lycanthropy; but he is using his abilities to help people.

"Do you really think werewolves are the worst things out there? If they learn control, they can remain mostly themselves during their change. This allows them to protect, not destroy, the humans that live in their community.

"Anyway, where was I," Jeff asked, getting a hold of himself once again. "Rowland will regret what he did to Rudi. He won't really punish him for reacting badly to the situation tonight. Rowland will know that Rudi thought that you were in danger and forgive him.

"We are almost to the hospital. Anything that you still have questions about?"

Darvis thought it over for a few seconds. Finally, he asked, "Will Rudi still be able to serve on the force after he goes through the change?"

"Close to his first full moon he will need to burn a few vacation days. Otherwise he will be the same guy he was before becoming a werewolf."

Jeff was impressed with the way that Darvis seemed to take the news that werewolves existed; and that one of his fellow officers would be becoming a werewolf himself. "The only thing that may change with Rudi is his temper. Werewolves can be easily angered. "

"Shit, that doesn't sound much different than the way the kid already was," Darvis commented. He and Jeff shared a laugh as they pulled in to the hospital.

While Darvis was getting Rudi, who was starting to stir, out of the backseat, he heard his Captain swear from behind him. Darvis glanced over his should to see Rowland, and another man he took to be Brian, heading over to them. They had, at least, had the decency to put some clothes on before came out to play in public.

"How'd they beat us here," Darvis questioned while his heart started to pound in his chest.

"We jogged of course," replied Brian while they approached. He had a grin on his face that said innocent. Darvis of course wasn't fooled by it. The man may be smaller than his alpha, but the look in his eyes was cold and didn't match the grin he wore.

3: The Alpha's Plight

e came to make sure the new pup survived," Rowland stated. He seemed to be a different person then he was before. Almost a comforting presence that was nothing like the dangerous air he held not even an hour earlier. "I'm sorry for the way I acted earlier. I was caught up in the packs celebration after our hunt tonight. The newest of us finally caught their first deer.

"I was already close to losing control when he tried to stun me. I'm just thankful that I regain a bit of myself at the sight of you, Jeff. Thank you for keeping me from doing something unforgivable. I couldn't stand if I took an innocent man's life."

"I know you well enough to know that you would have stopped yourself before killing him." Jeff was watching his friend without anger. Rather, Jeff appeared to sympathize with the way that Rowland was feeling. "Don't beat yourself up over this Rowland. Rudi will be thrilled to join your pack."

The young rookie looked confused at the last comment. "What's going on? I don't remember anything after we pulled up at that party," Rudi complained.

"Don't worry Rudi. Rowland and Brian will explain everything to you when you're ready to hear it," said Jeff as he walked with Rudi and Darvis over to where the other men stood. "You will have time to make adjustments before your first full moon. It's three weeks away."

"Actually it's more like sixteen days away," corrected Brian. "We have a built in moon detecting system. Kinda like a wolf sense. You know, like Spiderman, only cooler. No tights." Laughing at himself, he extended his hand toward Darvis to introduce himself. "I'm Brian Roberts."

"Hey, it's nice to meet you Brian. My name is Shawn Darvis. Though, everyone has called me Darvis since grade school," Darvis explained, taking the other man's hand in a firm hand shake. He could tell right away that Brian was struggling not to use too much strength when shaking his hand. Darvis wondered how strong werewolves were exactly; and what other gifts they may possess.

Brian, like Rowland, was only around six feet tall. He was muscular in build, but wasn't very large. In fact, he looked harmless. From his sandy blonde hair to his light blue eyes he just gave off the vibe that he wouldn't harm a fly. His hair cut short in military fashion, along with the way he moved when he walk, gave away the fact that he had spent years training to fight with deadly accuracy.

Rowland turned to Darvis than, with apologetic eyes. "I'm sorry for the way things went earlier. I hope that you can forgive me for what I did. By the way, it is truly nice to meet you, Darvis. Jeff talks about you quite often. In fact, I'm surprised that I hadn't met you before tonight."

"Um, it's ok, I guess. And it's nice to meet you as well," Darvis said, straining to remain polite. "I'm just glad that Rudi will be ok."

Bewildered, Rudi asked, "What are you guys talking about? I feel fine. Actually, I feel better than fine. I feel stronger and healthier than I have in years. In fact, I'm not sure I have ever felt this good in my life."

It was Brian who answered the question while everyone else seemed like they were at a loss for words. Of course Brian knew that Rowland was never at a loss for words. "Kid, listen. You got your throat ripped out about an hour ago by this guy," Brian told Rudi while jabbing his thumb in Rowland's direction. "He may not look like much, but he's the big bad wolf."

"Knock it off Brian," Rowland commanded with the slightest hint of a growl in his voice. At his words, Brian became silent and bowed his head.

Rudi looked as though he had received a blow at the tone Rowland used in his order to Brian. That's when Rudi felt a weird buzzing in the back of his mind. Then, he heard Brian's voice inside his head, 'Hey kid. He just doesn't want me saying anything in front of the others. Stop making that face like your hearing voices.' At Brian's orders, Rudi's face went relaxed and casual.

'Is that better? I didn't realize that I was making a face like I was hearing voices,' commented Rudi.

'Yeah, that's fine. Anyway, you had tried to use your taser on Rowland; which wasn't very wise. We werewolves are very....'

'Hold up! Did you just say that you guys are werewolves?' Laughing at how ridiculous it sounded to think it, Rudi realized it had to be true.

'As I was saying, we are very strong and not easily injured. All you managed to do was piss Rowland off. This is kind of impressive; since he never loses control over anything. I don't even get that much rise out of him and I try myself often. Though, being second in the packs chain of command has its perks. That and Rowland and I have been good friends for years. Even before he came out of the closet; and I don't mean as a werewolf.'

Brian and Rudi both glanced at Rowland and started laughing. It didn't take Rowland long to realize that Brian had been using his telepathy to talk to Rudi. However, it was the fact that he obviously had been talking about him that was annoying the hell out of Rowland. But, as usual, he didn't get angry with his friend. He'd think of something far worse to do to Brian than offer violence. I mean, Brian is the damn enforcer for the pack. The guy lives for violence. Even though Rowland knew that the guy was actually a very sensitive, kind hearted individual. 'What's so funny Brian? Did you make your usual crack about me being a homosexual just now?' Rowland projected at his second.

'I have no idea what you are talking about there Mr. Alpha, sir.' And, at his own witty remark that hadn't been heard by anyone other than Rowland, Brian fell to the pavement laughing.

Jeff and Darvis exchanged an inquisitive look at what was going on. Jeff shrugged at Darvis to let the other man know that he had no clues as to what was so funny.

Finally, after a minute to process what Brian had told him, Rudi spoke aloud. "So, are you telling me that I'm going to become a werewolf? Like, you know, go hairy at the light of the full moon and shit?"

Rowland was the one to respond. "Yes Rudi, you will become one of us. And yes we get hairy by the light of the full moon. Though, the moon doesn't hold as much sway as legend claims. Actually, we can change when we want to. Sometimes when we don't want to if we let our emotions get the better of us. Anger is the worst, and werewolves are naturally short tempered. None of us has figured out why that is exactly. My theory is that the beast that resides within us is temperamental because it wants to be in control more often. That's why I make my pack transform more often, and it seems to help with their control. Well, all of them except Brian. He's a bit insubordinate at times."

Looking at his alpha with false hurt on his face, Brian exclaimed, "Me? What about Ashlee? He never listens and doesn't know when to shut the fuck up!"

"Calm down Brian, I was only joking," said Rowland. Rowland enjoyed teasing his second in command about being insubordinate because it compares him to Ashlee. Ashlee is the lowest wolf in the pack and he doesn't have the sense to follow orders. Ashlee is the only wolf that Brian frequently has to punish. He acts like he enjoys punishing the guy, but Rowland knows that Brian hated having to hurt anyone.

"I know that you were joking," Brian said mater-of-factly. "I can read minds for Christ sake. Though, I don't like to pry information from people without permission."

"Oh, that's what was going on," Darvis exclaimed with awe in his voice. "I thought you three were just crazy when ya'll were laughing for no apparent reason. Guess that answered the question I had about what other things werewolves could do."

"Actually," Rowland explained. "Most werewolves don't have any abilities other than the heightened senses, increased strength and speed, oh, and my favorite, increase in sexual allure. But for some reason, the freaks of our kind seem to be drawn to my pack. By freaks, I mean werewolves with bonus abilities. Take Brian for instance. He has telekinesis and telepathy both. We have another that has this awesome ice vision thing. It's cool, literally."

"That has got to be the coolest thing I had ever heard of! Do you think that I might develop one of those special gifts," Rudi wondered. "Maybe I could have something cool like x-ray vision. Then I could go to the local university and check out the co-eds."

"Rudi, you're an idiot," Darvis said, rolling his eyes. "They wouldn't let you on any campus based on looks alone. Not to mention the fact that you give off that creeper vibe." Everyone laughed at the last part, even Rudi who was too dumb to know that the statement was supposed to be an insult.

"I may be a creeper, but at least I'm getting some," Rudi teased.

"I'm married you half wit! I love my wife, Sheila. She's beautiful and funny and smart and…"

"Not putting out any more," Rudi said interrupting Darvis before his rant about how great his wife was could continue.

Darvis glared at the younger man, but didn't say anything else. He realized then how tired he was. He looked at his watch and was shocked that it was going on eight am. He had been off duty for almost two hours. Guess time flies when you're getting the shit scared out of you by monsters that shouldn't really exist. "I think I'm going to head home. I'm bushed. Jeff, you mind giving me a ride back to my squad car?"

"Sure, be right there," Jeff promised. "Anyway, Rudi, you go with Rowland and get things worked out. Take care, Rowland. Brian."

"Later Jeff," Rowland and Brian said at the same time. And they watched as Jeff got back behind the wheel and pulled away.

"So, are you tired Rudi?" Rowland looked at the young man the way a father looked at his son. In a sense, Rudi realized, Rowland had become something of a father to him. The guy had created the new Rudi after all.

"No, sir. I'm way too excited about the prospect of becoming a werewolf to be able to sleep now. Though, I probably should get some rest," Rudi realized as his adrenalin started to ebb after such an exciting last few hours.

"Brian will take you home so that you can rest. However, when you wake-up, you have to call me," Rowland ordered, handing Rudi his card.

"I will. Talk to you when I wake-up than."

"Take it easy kid." And Rudi and Brian turned to leave.

'As if my pack hadn't gotten big enough in the few months since my change, now I have another wolf to look after. At least it will be nice to have someone in the pack with police connections,' Rowland thought to himself after he saw Brian's truck turn the corner.

Once the others were out of sight, Rowland turn and, in a burst of speed close to mach three, he too left the hospital parking lot. He headed for the closest stretch of woods and disappeared into the foliage.

4: Rudi Meets the Pack

fter a quick power nap, Rowland woke feeling refreshed. The problems of the night before seemed to have been no more than a dream. Of course Rowland knew that it was impossible for it to have been a dream because werewolves didn't have dreams. It was one of the more annoying side effects to the change. The only wolves that do have dreams are the ones that dream the future; which, of course, wasn't one of Rowland's talents.

Rowland went downstairs to grab a cup of coffee and have a bowl of cereal. He enjoyed the peace and quiet of his own home. This was rare, since the pack seemed to pop in and out as they pleased. It's not that he didn't love his extended family; he just liked time to himself. Especially since the pack tended to pop in more frequently when he had company of his own. By company, he was of course referring to his boyfriend, Stephen Mathews. Rowland knew that is was a matter of time before he would need to take the next step with Stephen and move in together. It helped that he already knew Rowland's deep dark secret. Wouldn't want something like that hanging over your head if you have your significant other move in.

Stephen was a fifth grade teacher at Albany Elementary. He was actually a few years older than Rowland was himself. He was just shy of the six foot mark and was kind of overweight. Though, it was only noticeable when he didn't have his shirt on. Otherwise, he looked to be in good shape. This didn't matter to Rowland, since love was always an irrational thing. Oh, and he was still human. Stephen didn't even try talking Rowland into turning him, much. Rowland knew the day would come when he would have to decide to turn the man or let him continue to grow old while Rowland himself barely aged. Perk of being a werewolf was long lives. Well, that was if you didn't get shot or stabbed by silver, or eaten by a bigger monster. Not exactly immortal, but living a few hundred years may have people thinking that the wolves are up there with creatures like vampires. Which, by the way, are a real pain in the ass for Rowland and his pack. There isn't a vampire Kiss in Albany, but there is one in the county.

Rowland had actually met Stephen through his sister, Kristie. Like her brother, she too was a teacher at Albany Elementary. The difference was, she taught Kindergarten. Oh, and she is Stephen's twin. She was the first wolf that Rowland had turned. Kristie is taller than her brother, standing at an even six foot. She had blonde hair and a well developed body, which only had gotten better when she went through the change. She, like nearly all of Rowland's higher ranking wolves, had special gifts. She could transform quicker than any other member of the pack, Rowland included. She also had an ability which she called the Sonic Howl. She is one wolf you don't want to have screaming at you. Let's say her bark is far worse than her bite. Though, the bite isn't anything to laugh about. Rowland knew about this ability all too well, since she learned of it while in an argument with him. He was thankful for rapid regeneration, otherwise he'd be deaf. Oh, and she is totally in love with Brian. Of course, Brian is completely clueless to this fact. For a psychic, he seems to lack insight.

Rowland stepped into the kitchen to find that coffee had already been brewed. He sniffed the air to see if he could detect who had been in his house. Not that he thought it was someone he didn't know. Thieves tended to just rob you, not make you coffee. He knew that it had been Ashlee as soon as he took a breath. Though, with the amount of foot traffic his place sees, it's a wonder that even his super charged sniffer could pick out one scent.

Ashlee and Rowland had once been best friends. However, that changed when Ashlee became a werewolf. Though, their friendship had been on the decline for a while; Rowland had just tried over looking it. He wasn't very powerful and Rowland knew that he blamed him for that. Add that to the fact that Ashlee was jealous of the bond that Rowland and Brian shared, and you get some problems developing between friends.

It didn't surprise Rowland that Ashlee had just let himself in and helped himself to coffee; and apparently, a ham sandwich as there was still a partial sandwich uneaten on the counter. Ashlee had always kind of helped himself to everything of Rowland's. Not that Ashlee returned the favor in kind. Rowland, however, never really cared, he always thought of Ashlee as a brother. Yet, when it came to Ashlee's pack rank, Rowland couldn't help being hard on him. I was the nature of the beast to treat lower wolves as such. Though, he went out of his way to keep Ashlee from being punished as often as possible. If he'd learn to keep his trap shut, Rowland wouldn't have to ever have him punished at all.

He decided not to go in search of Ashlee until after he ate breakfast and had his cup of coffee. It took a lot to piss Rowland off, but Ashlee may get that accomplished today. Especially if Rowland spoke to him before he had a bit of caffeine in his system. Not that caffeine works on a werewolf very well, a werewolf has to high of a metabolism to get a good caffeine buzz.

He settled down at the table with his cup of overly sweetened and heavily creamed coffee. He poured himself a bowl of Frosted Flakes. Frosted Flakes had always been one of Rowland's favorite breakfast cereals. Even though the box had an oversized cat with an ascot on, Frosted Flakes were still "Grrreat!"

He ate his cereal in rapid succession; not wanting the flakes to get soggy. After finishing the cereal itself, Rowland downed the bowl of cereal sweetened milk before even touching his coffee. He had eaten so quickly that the coffee was still piping hot.

Rowland savored the first taste of his master coffee making ability. Ok, no one else liked the way he made his coffee, but Rowland loved it. Before Rowland could enjoy a second savory taste of the warm caffeine filled goodness that his cup contained, Ashlee walked into the kitchen. He was the tallest of all the wolves in Rowland's pack. He stood a height of almost six foot five. He had medium brown hair that was blonde in the summer time because he spent his time in the sun. He rarely wore a shirt because he was in love with himself and liked to show his year round tan. Rowland was the only one that knew it wasn't natural. Can you say fake bake? Rowland never complained about the view; however, Ashlee's arrogance was what got him in trouble most to the time. Even before he begged Rowland to change him, Ashlee had a very well developed body. He had thought for sure he would have been a strong enough wolf to become second in the pack and bump Brian down. Of course, he'd been wrong. He never got that it wasn't just physical strength that made a dominant wolf; but their ability to protect as well as care for those weaker than themselves.

"Hey there boss man," Ashlee said to announce his entrance. Ashlee, not only was one of the wolves in Rowland's pack, but the receptionist at his office as well. "What's on the agenda for today?"

"Well, the new wolf should be coming by sometime today for a meeting with the pack. Then, I was thinking of taking him running to see if he is progressing normally," Rowland explained. He noticed that Ashlee seemed eager at the mention of a new wolf.

"Alright! Now I won't be the lowest wolf in our pack."

"Ashlee, you know it doesn't work that way. For all we know, Rudi could be more powerful than even I am." Rowland knew from how Rudi was progressing already that he would be no slouch in his pack. That would mean Ashlee remained the low dog in the pack. Though, Rowland did doubt that Rudi would prove to be powerful enough to be in the top three spots of the pack. Brian, Kristie, and Rowland himself were three of the most powerful wolves that Rowland had ever come across.

Shortly after he changed for the first time, Rowland had search the continental United States to find answers to what he had become. He learned quickly that he was a natural alpha. Even in some of the other packs he came across, Rowland had sway over their members. Sometimes he even could command other alphas, which he learned should be an impossible feat. Later, Rowland came across a powerful pack that had heard of an ability such as his. They referred to it as the "Alphas Call" ability.

It was when one of the wolves from that pack decided to challenge Rowland in order to prove the others wrong about this strange ability that Rowland noticed he had another special gift. This gift was formidable because it was both offensive and defensive. He could shoot ice beams from his eyes. Strange as it sounds, his opponent was frozen in place when he was about to pounce. From that day on, when Rowland was in his completed wolf form, his eyes were an icy blue that none of the other wolves he had come across had. Intrigue at his newest power, he set out on his return to Albany, practicing every chance he got.

Ashlee shook Rowland, bringing the man back to the present. "Did you hear me Rowland," Ashlee asked. He knew the answer to his question before he had asked it. Rowland often let his mind wonder these days. This could have been a bad thing if Ashlee himself would have been a more powerful wolf. Of course, the fact that he and Rowland were good friends would have kept him from attacking. Ashlee often wondered if Rowland would even be able to hold his own in a real fight with Brian, should Brian ever want to challenge their leader. In wolf form, there was no doubt that Rowland would serve Brian his ass on a silver platter, but in human form Brian was very lethal. "I was wondering if Rudi had shown any signs that he would be powerful or not. But your eyes glazed over before I even got a word out. Where do you go in that head of yours all the time lately?"

"Just thinking about things. Don't worry about it."

"Wouldn't you worry if it were me that was spacing out so often as of late? Talk to me, you know that I'm here for you," Ashlee pleaded with his alpha. "You have made me open up for years when I didn't want to. Even before you had the ability to make me tell you things. It's your turn to talk to me about the shit that's going on in that oversized brain of yours."

"You're right," Rowland said after a pause. He realized Ashlee had a point. He always made all of his friends confess what was bothering them. They tended to be annoyed by how observant he was when it came to their thoughts and emotions. Brian may be psychic, but Rowland was still better at reading those that were close to him. "I was just remembering when I first learned of my special gifts. About how scared and excited I was to learn that I had them. And how sorry I am that you didn't receive any bonus abilities; or a high rank in our pack."

"Oh, I don't know about not having any bonus abilities," Ashlee replies; trying to help convince Rowland that he really wasn't bitter with him for his lack of extra powers as a werewolf. He was just glad to be a part of the pack. "I think I have a few special gifts that you hadn't thought about."

"Really? Why haven't I sensed them?"

"Well, they aren't powers per say," Ashlee explained. "The first is that I'm more resistant to your orders than any other wolf in our pack, and most of the ones that you came across in your travels. Unless you really use your Alpha Call to its full potential, I still retain my free will.

Considering I didn't take orders from you very well before you changed me, I wasn't surprised to find that I could resist you still."

"That's very true, and possible the most annoying thing about you," Rowland joked. "What other gift do you have then?"

"The ability to annoy the hell out of Brian. He doesn't have the confidence that I have about almost anything, especially when it comes to women," Ashlee noted.

"I don't think is a lack of confidence on Brian's behalf when it comes to himself and women. He has always been less of a slut than you are Ashlee," Rowland began pointedly. "He, unlike you, treats women with respect. He wants to find a good girl that he can settle down with, not some piece of ass that he can text on a whim to come over. Besides, look at your track record. Most the women you end up with aren't attractive in the slightest."

"Not all of them are unattractive," Ashlee said, coming to the defense of his own ego.

"I said most of them were unattractive," Rowland corrected Ashlee. The fact that Ashlee got so defensive at the mention of the lack of good looking women he had bedded made Rowland happy. "I'm sorry. I just have to shoot down your ego a bit now and then. Wouldn't want that already swollen head of yours to explode."

Ashlee's face became very red and he was clinching his fists. However, before he could speak or attack, the door bell rang. 'It's me,' Brian projected into Rowland's mind. 'Rudi's with me. I see that Ash-hole is here already. This should be fun.'

'Just come in. And try not to start anything with Ashlee today.'

A few seconds later Brian walked into the kitchen flanked by a nervous and excited looking Rudi. The kid seemed to have put on at least fifteen pounds of muscle since Rowland had seen him that morning. Rowland could tell right away that Rudi would be unsurpassed in strength by any of his wolves when he completed the change. Rowland chanced a glance at Ashlee to see that he had noticed the same. Yet, knowing Ashlee as well as he did, Rowland knew that he wouldn't back down from the younger man. Ashlee thought for some reason that he had to prove himself against everyone. Especially when those people were nearly twice his size. No one said the guy was bright. If they did, it was a complete lie. Well, ok, he's not that dumb, but you would never guess by the shit he says.

"Reporting for duty sir," Rudi belted eagerly. Clearly the kid wanted to make a good first impression on his alpha. Rowland already liked the kid, even if the whole sir thing annoyed him because it made him feel old. "So, what do we do first?"

'Did you tell him to call me sir,' Rowland asked Brian with his mind. Judging by the smirk that Brian wore, the answer was a yes. Brian knew how much being called sir irked him. Projecting a mental roll of his eyes, Rowland continued aloud. "Well, first, let me introduce you to Ashlee. He and I have been friends for years. And I'm sure he will make you feel welcome."

Snorting with a quick burst of laughter, Brian said, "Yeah, I just bet Ash will make you feel very welcome."

"Brian, don't go starting shit now."

Ashlee couldn't help himself. He had to try to one up Brian in front of the new guy. "Yeah Brian. Don't start shit with me today. I'd hate to have to show you up in front of the new guy." Ashlee's laughter was cut short by a blow to his solar plexus that happened so quickly he didn't have a chance at dodging it. Brian apparently didn't care for the low wolf giving an open challenge to him. Rowland was glad that Ashlee hadn't finished the challenge that he almost had made. Wouldn't want blood all over his kitchen. Not to mention the whining that Ashlee was sure to make when healing.

"Please, can you two just get along for one day?" To Rudi this sounded like a simple question, but he felt the weight of an order hidden within the normal tone that Rowland had used.

"Yeah yeah," Ashlee said as if not affected by the command at all. Rowland just rolled his eyes at him. Rowland would get even with him for acting like this in front of Rudi. He wanted the new guy to feel welcome, not threatened.

"I'm sorry Rowland," Brian apologized. Rowland always liked that about Brian. He, unlike Ashlee, wouldn't let his pride get in the way of him apologizing to his friends when he had done wrong by them, or just pissed them off. Ashlee, however, thought that he was above having to say sorry to a friend. Though he thought his friends should be endlessly kissing his ass when they did something to anger him, no matter how small.

"Thank you, Brian. I just want Rudi's first day with the pack to go smoothly. Did you get a hold of everyone?" Rowland was eager to get the meeting over with. He had planned to take Rudi out, along with Brian and Kristie, to test what the kid was already capable of doing.

"Just got off the phone with Olivia when we pulled up. I was getting ready to call Ashlee, but I smelled his weak ass a block away," Brian said with glance at Rowland to make sure that he wasn't going to strike him upside the head for getting one more gibe in before the others showed up. "The others should be arriving shortly."

"What? You told the pack's bitches before you were going to tell me about the meeting," Ashlee began. He was clearing trying to act more hurt by this than he was. Rowland wondered if Ashlee thought that he would side with him and punish Brian for not telling Ashlee before the pack's females. Of course that would never be the case in his pack.

It was Rowland who responded to Ash's question. "You know that we do everything by rank in my pack, not by gender. If you started taking things more seriously in the pack, instead of expecting that you would have a higher rank, without any effort, because of your relationship with me as a friend; maybe a few of the others would end up actually being weaker than you. I don't want to upset you," Rowland said when, for the first time months, he saw real pain in Ashlee's eyes. "Ash, you just need to take a bit of responsibility for the way you act some times. Taunting the second in the chain of command is not the best way to do that."

"I know," Ashlee said while tear welled in his eyes. "I hate being the weak one all of the time. When I was still human, I looked small, yet I was actually a lot stronger than I looked. Now, as a werewolf, I look bigger than most of the pack; and I'm the weakest among us. My life just seems to suck all of the time, no matter what species I am."

"Dude, don't get so down on yourself. I can train you some. Then you won't be the lowest in the pack," Brian offered. He was always going out of his way to help friends. Even friends that he would barely consider a friend at all. Ones like Ashlee that is. "It will be tough, but I can get you to be the strongest of the submissive wolves. Who knows; your beasts nature may even alter to that of a dominant."

"You would do that for me? Even though I am usually a dick to you,"

Ashlee chocked out through the tears that had started to leak from his eyes.

"Of course I will. Our pack is only as good as it's weakest member. That would mean ours was very weak and shitty if you remain the weakest," Brian blurted out of habit. "What I mean is that you can be better. I know that for a fact. So, quit crying."

"Gee, thanks. I think."

"Well, that was touching guys," Rowland said. He was starting to feel all gushy after Brian and Ashlee's little truce. He knew it wouldn't last. Ashlee would have Brian train him, Rowland was sure of that. However, Ashlee wouldn't take it seriously. Then Brian would beat him within an inch of his life, again. "I heard some of the others pull in. Let's make our way to the living room to greet them."

The first to arrive was Kristie. Though, Rowland was shocked to see that she had her brother in tow. As Rowland's mate, Stephen was allowed to be at any of the pack's meets. Technically, Stephen could have as much head way in the pack as Brian did, if he wished to play the role of the alpha's mate. Yet, he usually tried to keep out of pack business. That was his sister's thing, not his.

They were followed shortly by Nick, Dylan, Sherry, Justin, and Kimberly. The five of which were the other dominant wolves in the pack. Though, only Dylan, Justin, and Kimberly had extra gifts. Dylan had the gift that complimented Rowland's own ice vision. He of course had the ability to shoot jets of fire from his eyes. Heat vision as it had begun to be called. Justin could levitate. He couldn't quite fly. Well, not yet anyway, but he was hopeful. Kim, well she had one of the most powerful gifts that a wolf could hope for. She had command of nature. That included plants and some animals. It's no wonder the pack had began to call her "Mother Nature."

The last to show were Zach, Phillip, Wyatt, Leslie, and Olivia. The five submissive that still out ranked Ashlee.

"Everyone, I'd like to introduce you to Rudi." Rowland said as the last members of the pack strolled into the living room. "Rudi, I'd like to introduce you to the pack," Rowland began the introductions in order of rank in the pack; he pointed at them as he said their names. "You already know Brian. This here is Stephen. He is my mate, thus he has a high standing in the pack; even though he's still human. And the woman to his left is Kristie; she is the pack's third and Stephen's sister."

"It's a pleasure to meet you," said Stephen and Kristie at the same time. Sometimes it seemed that the twins shared more than similar features. Maybe they had a mental link with one another, Rowland thought. That would explain why they are the only two people whose minds Brian couldn't touch. Whatever it was, Rowland found it kind of creepy when they did the talking at the same time thing.

"Like wise," Rudi said politely.

"Next would be the lovely Ms. Kimberly," Rowland continued. "She is the fourth in the pack. You will find out very soon why that is. The fifth in line is Dylan. Sixth is Justin. Then comes Sherry and Nick. That concludes the dominant wolves of our pack. Well, the dominant ones we have so far anyway. But I wouldn't be very surprised to see you shoot up the ranks quickly, Rudi. You seem to be showing great potential.

"And lastly, we have the glue that holds our pack together. Without the submissive wolves, we would have a lot of fighting within the pack. They help us keep balance and, in my opinion, are the backbone of werewolf society," Rowland told Rudi. He wanted the kid to understand how important it was to have submissive members. "Those members are Wyatt, Phillip, Leslie, Zach, Olivia, and of course Ashlee.

"It is the responsibility of all of the dominant wolves to protect the submissive. Not that they need protecting from humans, no offense Stephen," Rowland added with a glance at the other man.

Stephen smiled to Rowland and added, "You know they really should need protection from me. If they piss me off, they have to deal with your wrath." Rowland and Stephen shared a laugh at that comment.

"This is true," interjected Rowland, getting back to the topic at hand. "I'm meant normal humans. Anyway, where was I?"

Rowland was always distracted when Stephen was near. He felt human again for those precious seconds when he locked eyes with Stephen. He wondered often if he would have less control had he not been involved with his boyfriend. His rage that lurked below the surface so often seemed to fade to the tiniest blip on his emotional radar when his other half was around.

"Ah, that's right, protecting the submissives," Rowland continued after giving himself a mental shake to clear his wondering mind. He chanced a glance at Ashlee to find him studying his face very carefully. He could see that he was the only one, with the exception of Brian who could literally read his thoughts, who noticed that his mind had wondered so far away for that split second. One plus to being a werewolf is that their minds processed information quickly.

'Not all of us have minds to process information with,' Brian sent Rowland with a very sly smirk spread on his face. Rowland couldn't help the small burst of laughter that overwhelmed him at the remark. He did not need to have Brian say who he was insinuating was a brainless oaf. Ashlee was the only wolf Rowland had ever met that didn't show any acceleration in his thinking process. Of course, Ashlee never went out of his way to think when others would do it for him.

"It is from other supernatural beings that we must protect the submissive wolves," Rowland finally finished.

"Wow, that sounds like it's going to be hard to remember everyone's rank and what responsibilities the dominants have toward the lower ranking submissive ones," Rudi stated. He was beginning to think that he may not be cut out for all these wolf politics. There seemed to be so many rules already and he hadn't even gone through the change.

"Don't worry kid," Brian said. He had been listening in on the thoughts of everyone in the room to try and get an advanced warning if someone had a problem accepting Rudi in the pack. "Most of the wolf stuff will be more instinct than rules. Rules are a human invention to make people feel suppressed. We werewolves are free. The rank stuff you will be able to sense after the change is complete. You will even know if you are more dominant than someone else. Of course, we do have rules for fighting for rank that we will discuss with you when they come up. As for protecting the subs, you won't even have to think about it. It's imbedded in your genetics now."

"Well, shit, this should be a blast than. I joined the force to be able to protect people. Now I'm going to be protecting more than just the people in my community. We're kinda like superheroes."

"I don't know if we could call ourselves superheroes," Kristie said, speaking for the first time. Rudi noticed that her voice held an air of authority to it. He was under the impression that it must be a wolf thing. However, the rest of the pack knew it was a teacher thing. "We try to just mind our own business when the supernatural community is concerned. Why risk our lives unless we absolutely have to."

"Well Kristie, if Rudi wants to use his new found abilities to help protect innocents, then that's his choice," Rowland told the woman. He felt that it was actually a good idea for them to be using their gifts to protect others. As soon as their control was good enough, which, for some could take months. He knew in that moment that Rudi would end up being a hero once he tamed the beast within as much as possible. "In fact, I think that we should protect all of the people in our community from the things that go bump in the night"

"Hello! Bad things don't just come out at night," Ashlee pointed out. More to be a wise ass than informative, thought Rowland.

"It's a figure of speech, jackass. You really should learn to keep your smart ass mouth shut," shouted Rowland, growing very tired of Ashlee and his snarky attitude for the day; and the day had only just started for him.

Everyone backed away from Rowland at that moment; with the exception of Stephen who had moved closer to him. Rowland's eyes had turned the glowing blue they get when he's on the verge of losing control to the beast, for the second time in less than twenty-four hours. He was shaking with a rage he himself had only seen in the other members of his pack. It was beginning to worry him that he was finally losing the impressive control he had over his inner wolf. He could feel his bones and muscles begin to shift when he felt a warm, soothing hand on his shoulder.

"Just breath," Stephen told him. "We are all here for you. You're going to be alright. I will never leave you, no matter what."

Rowland could tell that he would always be by his side. He wished that no one but Stephen were there right then. He felt like breaking down, but couldn't do that in front of the others. Showing that much weakness could be fatal if the others lost control.

When Rowland finally looked at the other people still in his living room, there were a few of them that looked as if they too were about to lose control. He knew that it was his own beast that was calling to theirs. If Stephen hadn't been there, the town could have been in grave danger.

Rowland decided that Ashlee had gone way to far this time. He was obviously too lenient on him. That was about to change. 'Brian, Christmas is coming early for you. You finally get to dish out a nice beating on Ashlee. That was way to close.'

'Um, thank you. Though I'm still not clear on way you lost control. Ashlee has done way worse things than this and you didn't flip your lid. Is everything alright? Your thoughts have seemed more distant lately.' Brian thought at Rowland. Worry lines were creased on Brian's forehead as he studied his friend.

'I'm not sure what has been wrong with me lately. However, you will be the first to know when I figure something out. I mean that literally, as soon as I think it you will know.'

"You shouldn't be making a joke of this," Brian said out load. Rowland felt bad that he had tried making a joke of the problem. Brian was his friend and worried that Rowland needed to talk; yet wouldn't. Rowland was one of the few people that could keep his thoughts hidden from Brian if he wanted to.

"I know. I'm just not sure what's going on anymore; and I hate not being in control of everything."

Rowland was really starting to get tired of having everyone there. He needed time to collect his thoughts before he lost it completely. "Okay. Meeting is adjourned," he finally said. "Kristie, you and the others take Rudi out running. I want you to fill me in on how he does and how you think he may rank when he does finally change. Brian, I would like you to stick around to talk."

Stephen started walking toward the door and Rowland grabbed his arm. "It's alright Rowland. I know that Brian will understand what's going on with you better than I could."

"Stephen, please don't go," Rowland pleaded with pain in his voice. "I need you here. I didn't mean for it to sound like I wanted only Brian to stay. Those were pack orders. I always want you to stay with me." Rowland leaned in and kissed Stephen on the cheek; and pulled him away from the door with his arm around his waist. Rowland was glad that all of his friends and pack were not disturbed by him expressing his affection toward Stephen in front of them. In fact, he was more uncomfortable with it than they were.

Kristie took all of this to be a sign that she needed to get the others out of there fast. She turned to the others and said, "Okay, you heard the man; let's get a move on."

She started following the others to the door with Ashlee by her side when she turned back to face the three men left in the room. "Will you fill me in on what's going on later?"

"Of course I will," Rowland assured her. "You and Ashlee both will be told what's going on as soon as we get this sorted out. You two are more like family to me than friends. I wouldn't dream of keeping something as potentially important as this from you."

At hearing this, Ashlee zoomed back to Rowland in a blur of speed. He threw his arms around his alpha in a friendly hug that took Rowland by complete surprise; and said, "I'm so sorry Rowland. Please forgive me. I love you bro."

"I love you too, Ash. And I know you're sorry." Rowland was sure he really was sorry, but he was not going to change his mind about Ashlee needing to be punished. "You two need to be going now." And the two of them vanished out the door.

"So," Rowland started, turning his attention to Stephen and Brian. "What would you guys say if I said that I have been feeling as if someone has been trying to invade my mind?"

Stephen and Brian exchanged a horror filled look of realization. Rowland knew from the terror that was on their faces that they weren't surprised to hear that he thought this was happening. Almost as if the both of them had come to the same conclusion when he did.

5: Hard Mind to Break

 see," Rowland said. He began to see how close he may have been to the truth in assuming that someone was messing with his brain. "So, you two had already figured out that there was an outside force messing with my mind?"

"Yeah. Brian and I thought there might be someone messing with you for a few days now." Stephen stepped closer to Rowland. Rowland knew that he was trying to assure him that he wasn't intentionally keeping things from him. No one would want the big bad wolf to get mad. He only wished he couldn't smell Stephen's fear as he approached. "I was hoping it wasn't true. But that does explain why your mind seemed to wonder so often lately. It's almost as if someone wants you out of the way. But why only you, we haven't figured out yet."

Brian stepped forward at that moment. "We think that you are being targeted because you are the alpha of one of the most powerful packs that any of us had ever heard of in the history of werewolf society. Of course that is only a guess."

It hurt Rowland to have two of the most important people in his life so worried about him. It reminded him of when he was young…

Rowland shock his head. He had never dwelled on his childhood before, why start now. And as he thought the question, the answer came to him. He felt the presence in his skull trying to keep him from focusing on the task at hand.

He pressed his mental defenses that had grown since he and Brian had been practicing on Brian's own ability. Though this was a less obvious invasion; Rowland finally found the intrusion. Unfortunately he wasn't able to trace it back to its master. "Brian, do you sense that? I don't want to push them out till you get a feel for their mind. Can you sense them close to the house? They can't be that far from here."

Brian concentrated on Rowland's mind for a long second. "Um, I can barely sense them in your thoughts. If you hadn't pointed them out to me, I would have missed it," Brian said in a voice shaky with the fear this powerful intruder had brought forth within him. Which was saying something if this being was strong enough to have Brian unnerved. "I can't sense him around the house at all. He must be miles away."

Stephen whistled at that realization. "Damn, this has got to be the most powerful psychic you have encountered so far. I wonder what he wants."

Rowland wasn't listening to either of them. Any time he tried to concentrate on the conversation; the mind that was touching his tried to take hold. He couldn't let that happen. He focused all of his mental might into an attack on the invader. He could tell that he had barely won the small mental battle with the guy that was after his mind.

After banishing the other from his thoughts for the time being, Rowland through up major mental shields that no one would get around. Even God himself would have trouble getting into those thoughts that Rowland hid behind solid steel. He wondered how much the strange presence had gotten from his thoughts. "Brian, you won't be able to talk mind to mind with me till after we find this guy. I can't let my defenses down for anything. Unless it's an emergency or I figure out a way to allow only your mind in "

"I understand completely. I felt how hard you had to fight against this guy. I thought I was a badass telepath, but my power seems weak and pathetic compared to this."

"What I don't get," Stephen said. "Is why you seem to snap out of it when I come close to you? I always thought I was your weakness."

"You are the one aspect in my life that keeps me sane. Without you I would be lost. It isn't a surprise to me that you give me the power to overcome this advisory," Rowland admitted, swelling with pride at how true the statement was.

Stephen looked into Rowland's eyes and it was obvious that he felt the same way. Brian cleared his throat to remind the two of them that he was still there. It was bad enough for him to hear and see what Rowland was thinking; he could so do without the live version. "What exactly are we going to do about this mental terrorist," asked Brian. Clearly he was the only one whose thoughts were still on the topic at hand. Of course, Rowland's mind had wondered to places he never wanted it to go to in his presence again. Does eeeew mean anything to him? At least he couldn't read what Stephen thought, not that he needed to read him. I'm sure it couldn't have been much different than the nasty thoughts going through Rowland's head. Realizing at that point Rowland had unintentionally dropped the shields he had just worked hard at constructing, Brian thought at him, 'You really should keep your mind on your shielding and out of the gutter.'

"Oh, shit. I'm sorry Brian. I didn't mean for you to see all of that," Rowland said out load. Then he added with his mind, 'I will try to keep my defenses up a bit stronger when you are around Stephen and me.' Rowland was so embarrassed that he had thought things like that around one of his best friends; let alone around the telepathic one.

"I'm going to need you to go into the city for a little talk with our informants at 'Candiland' to find out what they know. Grab my black book and call up Marzipan. I'm sure she will be expecting to hear from one of us soon. She tends to know way more than she should. Damn demon woman. But be careful around her, last time I barely got you out of there before you were her next snack," Rowland warned his second.

"I'm always careful. Maybe I should bring Ashlee with me," Brian said with a wicked glint in his eyes. "Marzipan would love him, and he would no doubt love her. He would make great cannon fodder."

"As much as you may be making a joke of this, I think that Ashlee would be great back up for you in this situation. He would distract Marzipan from using her powers as a succubus on you and allow you to press her for information," Rowland said as the wheels clearly continued to turn in his brain. "Before you ask, and I know you will; you can't leave Ashlee behind when you leave 'Candiland.'"

"Damn the luck. I was so hoping that we could get rid of two problems with on solution," Brian said. They all shared a laugh. "So, the number's in you black book."

Brian looked at the desk and squinted his eyes slightly. With a rush of air, the black book flew off the top of the desk to rest in Brian's hand. Rowland hated when Brian used his telekinesis around him, the buzzing of power was just annoying. Super senses are a bitch sometimes.

"Okay, I got her number," Brian said. "Now all I have to do is wait for my decoy to get back from his run."

"Brian, would it have killed you to take a few steps to pick the damn book up off the desk," Rowland asked the psychic boy wonder.

"Um, yeah. Why would I walk over there when this is so much faster? Plus, you tell us to practice our gifts as often as possible. Never know when some big nasty is going to come knocking on the door."

"Yeah, yeah. I think that you should take Darvis with you as well. It couldn't hurt having the police already there when the shit goes down; even it the club is completely out of his jurisdiction. And shit always goes down at that strip club," Rowland suggested. Though, he would make it an order if it wasn't carried out as he requested.

"Sure. I will get his number when Rudi gets back," Brian confirmed. He knew that he could say no. However, he hated when Rowland used the Alpha Call on him. He loved the guy, but it seemed wrong that he could take away his free will so easily.

Brian walked into the kitchen to use his cell phone to call Marzipan. Rowland watched as he left the room; then he turned to Stephen. "We have to be more careful around Brian. He may not be able to read your mind, but he can read mine like an open book when I'm not on guard. He's a great guy, but there is only so much that he can stand to see when it comes to you and I," Rowland said, feeling sympathetic toward his friend.

"I know. Sometimes it sucks that you have such gifted friends. Especially when it's the one that can get inside of your head, literally. I just wish that we didn't have to worry about all of that," Stephen told Rowland with the pain that hiding his nature from the world gave him plain on his face. Rowland and his pack never had Stephen suppress his true nature around them. However, the community of Albany, mainly the parents of his students, wouldn't take to kindly to the way he is.

Before they could finish their conversation, Brian yelled from the kitchen, "You two may want to finish up with your lovers spat. The rest of the pack will be back any minute. Thought you would appreciate the heads up. And don't worry, I did hear your conversation, but it's no sweat off my brow that you two were talking about me. It's not like either of you expected me to not hear."

A few seconds after Brian's warning, the rest of the pack began to file back into the house. Kristie was, of course, in the lead. Then, Rudi walked in next, still panting from his exertion, which *was* a surprise to Rowland. After Rudi, the rest of the pack began to pile into the house in the order of their rank. Rowland was impressed that Rudi must have been proven to be in the top five ranking spots of the pack already; and he wouldn't be changing for a little over a week. That was a scary thought. Of course, the ranking of the pack members was ever changing.

"What did you guys figure out while we were out," Kristie asked, wasting no time at all asking for the information she had missed when she took the pack running. She always went straight to the point when it pertained to pack business.

6: UP TO SPEED

efore I get into details of what we have discovered, I want to know how well Rudi did on his run," Rowland said to Kristie with a slight hint that he couldn't tell her in front of the entire pack just yet.

Kristie, being the very bright woman that she was, picked up on the hint easily and began reporting Rudi's progress. "Well, Rudi is going to become very powerful indeed. He is already as fast as most of the pack, with the exceptions being only Kim and myself. I could almost guarantee that he is going to have a powerful gift to boot. I felt energy, like static forming in his palms when he had gotten close to me. I'd wager his gift will be something like a bolt of lightning. He shows great promise of potential."

Before Rowland could say anything to this report, Rudi spoke up. The excitement at Kristie's words was clear in his voice, "You really think I could be that powerful? Gosh, that would be badass." Rudi was practically glowing with self pride. That was until Ashlee chimed in with his always unwanted remarks.

"Did you really just say 'gosh?' I mean, seriously, could you be any more childish. We are all grown-ups here, you could have said something a little less first grade-ish."

Apparently Rudi didn't like to be made fun of because he was on top of Ashlee within seconds, pinning him to the ground. Rowland had never seen a wolf, even one as weak as Ashlee, be over powered by some one that had yet to have their first full moon experience. It was very impressive to watch. However, Rowland couldn't let him hurt Ashlee to bad, even with the rapid healing, because he needed Ashlee to send with Brian to the strip club for information. So, in a fraction of a second, Rowland was across the room pulling Rudi off of Ashlee.

He used his alpha voice the calm both of the wolves. Otherwise, he would have ended up with one of them lying dead on the floor.

"I'm so sorry Rowland. I don't know what came over me," Rudi apologized.

It was Brian that answered the apology, "No sweat kid. Ash-hole has that affect on a lot of people. And the temper thing is all part of the changing process"

Brian then turned to Rowland, "Maybe you should talk to Jeff about having Rudi take a few weeks off till he gets the temper stuff under control a bit."

"I couldn't agree more," Rowland stated, glancing at Rudi. "Hey, what is Darvis' phone number? We need him to go with Brian and Ashlee on a trip to 'Candiland' to gather information."

"Um, let me check real quick," Rudi said, pulling his cell out of his pocket. He flipped open his phone and read off the number. "His number is 555-1763. But what kind of mission would you need him for?"

"One in which we require a police officer's insight on to help us figure out what we might be up against. That's all I can tell you right now," Rowland said to Rudi.

"What's this shit about Ashlee having to go? Don't I have a say in whether I go with Brian anywhere," Ashlee asked. He clearly didn't like having his plans made for him.

"Actually, you don't have a say in this," Rowland told him plainly. "Consider this your punishment for acting like a jackass earlier."

"YES SIR! Anything you say boss man," Ashlee said.

"You will learn someday to treat others with respect. I will make sure of it, trust me," Rowland growled at Ashlee with a dangerous sneer to add to the threat that was very clear in his voice.

Ashlee, for the first time that Rowland remember, cringed away from him in that moment.

"Brian, go call Darvis and see if he can go with you. Don't give him any information until you pick him up," Rowland directed.

"Sure thing. Then Ash and I will roll out," Brian said, disappearing into the kitchen once again to use the phone.

"Okay. The pack meeting is officially adjourned. Kristie, Kim, and

Dylan, stick around and I will fill you in on what is going on. Or what we think is going on at any rate. The rest of you may leave. That includes you, Ashlee. You will need to change for your trip to the city with Brian. Pack meeting on Thursday, don't forget." Rowland strolled over to the door to open it for his guest like a good host.

"See you Thursday Rowland," said Olivia and Wyatt as they left. The rest of the pack members just nodded their goodbyes and exited the house.

As soon as the others were out of ear shot, it was Dylan who spoke first. "Rowland, what's going on man? You have all of us on edge as of late. We are all starting to worry that there is something seriously wrong going on."

"No kidding. Even we, your strongest dominants, are starting to lose control more often. How could this happen? My gifts can be very dangerous if I lose control." No one would disagree with Kimberly on that. Having control of nature would make her very dangerous if she lost it.

"I think..." Rowland began until Stephen cleared his throat to correct him. "Fine, we think that someone is getting in my head, literally. The person, or whatever it is, has been turning my thoughts away from the present; and in the process, causing my control to fail. Whoever is doing this obviously doesn't want to pack to be aware of what they are up to. A scarier thought is that they are apparently gaining this much control over my mind and are still out of the range of Brian's telepathy."

"Your right, that is a scary thought," Kimberly said. Kim had always been the pacifist of the pack. She was a dominant without a doubt, but she avoided fighting when she could. This was why she, who had the most powerful gift of all of the pack's members, wasn't pack second. She has light brown hair, with blonde highlights, cut short in a pixie due. Her skin was that of a creamy milk chocolate. She was a slender woman, though she had nice definition because of the changes effects. Before the change, she was one of those women that one looks at and wonders how they could walk around outside when the wind was even barely blowing. However, as a werewolf, her small size gave her added speed that no other pack member could match. Rowland himself was the only member who could even get close to catching her when they were running full speed.

Kim had never really been interested in becoming a monster until her life was in jeopardy. She and Rowland had been out for a walk in the woods when she had seen an empty bird's nest that she thought was interesting near the top of a tree. She had started climbing up to retrieve it from its home. She was about twenty feet up when the branch snapped. She fell to the ground with bone crushing force. Her back had been broken. She had begged Rowland to kill her, which he couldn't do. Rowland may not take much crap from anyone; but he could not take another's life. So she settled for being changed into a monster.

"That's why you are sending Brian and Ash to visit Marzipan, isn't it? That explains you placing two straight guys in such danger from the succubus herself. Does Ashlee even know what she is," Dylan asked.

"Ash doesn't have a clue what she is or what she can do. If he knew, he would get the wrong idea about her and let his guard down. I'm leaving it up to Brian to keep him alive. Brian has never let me down before. Plus, Darvis is going to be with them. It couldn't hurt to have a cop around, could it?" Rowland was worried that he over estimated whether what little resemblance of friendship he had with Marzipan would be enough to keep them safe. It was like sending them into the lion's den. But Rowland himself would have been a liability at the moment, so he really didn't have much choice in sending others to do this for him.

"You have a point. Ashlee would throw himself at Marzipan if he heard that she was a kind of sex crazed demon. He's such a pervert sometimes," Dylan said. Dylan was the second youngest member of the pack. He was turned on his twenty-first birthday. He was around five foot ten inches tall. He had a natural muscle tone that was developed from years of working on a farm as a boy. He had dark brown hair that was wavy and hung to his shoulders. He works as a fireman when he isn't up to his elbows in pack politics.

In fact, it was because Dylan had suffered third degree burns over most of his body after being trapped inside of a burning house that Rowland had changed him. His burns healed almost instantly after Rowland infected him.

Rowland always wondered whether the special gifts that his pack members developed had anything to do with the reason that each individual had been changed. Dylan being injured in a fire and he developed heat vision. Kim falling out of a tree and she now controls nature. Hell, Rudi developing an electric ability would fit the pattern.

Since, he had been changed after trying to fry Rowland's ass with his stunner.

Brian walked out of the kitchen laughing. He had apparently thought Dylan's comment to be quite funny. "I'm taking off. I will call you on your cell as soon as we leave Candiland. I just hope that Ashlee is ready. He takes longer than a woman to get ready."

"Good luck. And try to be careful," Rowland said as Brian was walking out of the door. Brian just waved and then disappeared into the night.

"I just hope nothing happens to Brian on this little fact finding mission you are sending him on, Rowland." Kristie had worry etched plainly on her face when she said this.

"Sis. Why don't you just tell Brian that you have feelings for him? Everyone else notices the way you look at him; and the way that he looks at you in return. Are the two of you really so stupid that neither of you noticed," Stephen informed his sister. He was getting tired of watching the two of them doing the stupid flirting game with one another, so he decided to get involved.

Kristie just stuck her tongue out at her brother, though she knew that he was right. Brian wouldn't make a pass at her because he can't read her thought. She knew that he would be worried about being rejected.

"I think that we are all up to speed about the situation. I'm going to go over to Brian's dojo and train a bit. Have to focus on something while I wait for Brian and Ashlee to get their mission completed." Rowland walked out his own front door, leaving his guest still standing in his living room. He didn't care if they stayed there; he trusted all of his pack.

7: Death of a Sales Woman

rian pulled up to Ashlee's house and knew right away that the jackass wasn't ready yet. Telepathy has his perks sometimes. Not to mention that Brian could smell the shower from the driveway.

He walked up the little path made between bushes and when he reached the door, he just walked in without knocking. He knew that Ashlee had heard him pull up, so he didn't bother to announce his presence.

Ashlee walked out of the bathroom in nothing more than a towel. Instead of making his way to his bedroom, he walked into the living room where Brian waited. 'You know that you like seeing me in only a towel,' Ashlee projected at Brian. 'You may as well admit that you're gay. That is why Rowland favors you over me.'

'You are way more gay than I will ever be,' Brian retorted. 'Plus, I have seen in your thoughts that you have tried shit with Rowland. Maybe you should take your own advice and come out already.'

"Ouch! That's harsh. I'm sorry that I started the insults first, but you didn't have to resort to the time I got really drunk and may have tried shit with Rowland to finish the little argument," Ashlee said defensively. He and Brian always seemed to doubt the others sexual orientation. That, of course, was one of the main reasons in which they fought with each other. However, neither of them was truly gay at all.

"It's cool. Just go put some damn clothes on, please. I want to get this over with some time tonight. I will be in the truck when you're ready there, princess." And so Brian walked out of the house.

"Very funny," Ashlee called to Brian's back as he made his way outside. "You're the princess."

After he didn't get even the slightest rise out of Brian with his poor excuse for an insult, Ashlee finally went into his room to get dressed.

Brian waited impatiently for Ashlee to get done finding clothes for about fifteen minutes before Ashlee finally made his way out to the truck.

"What took you so long to get dressed?" Brian never understood why it took Ashlee so long to get ready. "Grab a shirt, pants, underwear, socks, and shoes and then you're done. It really isn't that complex."

"Are you kidding? I'm going out in public. Gotta look good for the ladies," Ashlee said, flipping down the visor to gawk at his reflection in the tiny mirror on the visor's reverse side. He was clearly in love with himself.

"You do realize that 'Candiland' is a gay bar right," Brian said jokingly.

"Screw that, I'm not going with you to some gay bar that Rowland wouldn't even go to himself," Ashlee said reaching for the handle of door to get back out of the truck.

"Dude, I was joking. It's a strip club, short bus," Brian told Ashlee. "We gotta get some information from the owner/stripper. But first we have to pick Darvis up at the police station."

Ashlee glanced at Brian. He wasn't sure whether Brian was joking about it being a strip club either. Ashlee never really cared for strip clubs himself, even though he was a big pervert. "So this strip club, how do you know this stripper that works there," Ashlee asked with a sheepish glint in his eyes.

"Her name is Marzipan. And I can honestly tell you that I wish I didn't know her. She isn't exactly human. She has been around since before the time of the pharaohs; the ruling body of ancient Egypt," Brian informed Ashlee.

"Really? That's one old bitch. She has got to be horribly wrinkly; and her boobs probably sag to the floor. How can people want to see her strip? It makes me nauseous thinking about it. What is she exactly?"

"She is a demon know as a succubus. They are nasty little things. Okay, they are actually the size of a normal human; but, whatever. The way they feed is interesting. Their food enjoys been consumed."

"Wow, that's nuts. What kind of a sick crazy ass mother fucker would enjoy being eaten," Ashlee wondered aloud.

Brian started laughing at how little Ashlee knew about demons and other supernatural beings, considering he was one of them. "Let's just say that she doesn't exactly eat you like normal. She fed a bit off of me before and I must say it felt, well, wow is all that comes to mind. If Rowland wouldn't have been resistant to her, um, charms, he and I would have both been completely consumed. Trust me, you will see what I mean. That's why I wear this necklace," Brian said, indicating the pentacle at the end of the chain around his neck. "It's for protection from demons. Her powers won't affect me when we get there."

"Where the hell is mine?" Ashlee was only starting to realize how dangerous their mission actually was.

"I only have one extra necklace and it would be better to have Darvis wearing it. He's only human after all."

"What about me? Doesn't my life mean jack anymore since I'm more than human?"

"Calm down Ash," Brian pleaded, trying to get Ashlee to not freak out. "I will be there to keep anything from happening to you. We have to do this to save our entire pack."

"Screw the pack. Haven't you ever heard of self preservation?"

"That is why you aren't a dominant. Always concerned with what happens to you, instead of trying to protect others. If we don't do this we may all die anyway; not to mention the deaths of countless innocent people. If Rowland loses control then the rest of his pack will. You are all too young to keep from rampaging without him around. Trust me, you don't want to know what it's like to see yourself killing the ones you love; and not be able to do a damn thing to stop it. I live with my nightmarish past and barely keep myself sane. I wouldn't wish that on anyone else," Brian told Ashlee while tears glistened in his eyes.

Ashlee was speechless. He knew that Brian's past was a mystery to almost everyone in the pack. The only pack member who knew what Brian had done in his past was Rowland. All Ashlee had known was that Brian was changed during a military experiment that had gone wrong. They had been trying to combine werewolf blood with soldiers to make then stronger and faster; not to mention that they would be nearly bulletproof. But they hadn't known just how little it took to trigger the change until it was too late. The only one that survived after the government decided that the newly turned wolves were a liability had been Brian.

Ashlee could only imagine the blood and carnage that the ex-marine had caused while escaping. He assumed that it hadn't been entirely the beast doing the killing during the escape. It took Ashlee a few seconds to realize that it was Brian's thought he was seeing instead of his own imagination. The horror was so vivid. Ashlee felt more sympathy for the man in the driver's seat than he had for any other person he knew.

Neither man spoke until they reached the police station. It was Brian that spoke first when he took his phone out of his pocket. "I gotta call Darvis to let him know that we are here," Brian told Ashlee, who still looked pale after seeing a bit of Brian's past. 'He should be glad I didn't show him the bad shit,' Brian thought while dialing his phone.

"Hey Darvis, it's Brian. We just got to the station. Where are you at?"

Though Brian's phone wasn't on speaker, or even turned up load for that matter, Ashlee could still hear the man on the other end of the line. "I'm inside talking to Jeff. You boys need to come in here. We may need your help with a murder that had taken place tonight."

The line went dead before Brian could get any more information about what Darvis had been talking about. "I just spoke to Darvis forty-five minutes ago. This murder must have just happened," Brian said to Ashlee, answering one of the many questions that were clear in Ashlee's face.

"Yeah. But why would they want to involve the pack?"

Brian remembered that Ashlee was a fairly new wolf and didn't know that he and Rowland had helped the police with strange cases before; not that anyone other than Jeff knew about it. Though, they didn't really have time to solve murders right now. "We sometimes help the cops with their strange cases," Brian stated simply.

"Oh," Ashlee replied.

Hopping out of the truck, Ashlee and Brian made their way to the police station's entrance. Brian had already started the thought process of wondering if this murder was connected to the mind invader that had been plaguing Rowland. It would be a big coincidence if it wasn't somehow connected. Brian never held much stock in coincidences.

Brian and Ashlee made their way into the station. Before either of them could ask to be buzzed in, one of the officers on duty already had the door open for them. Brian could already see the carnage of the woman's death inside of the officer's mind.

The woman had been attacked; and not by anything human. The claw markings were similar to that of a werewolf's. Brian stopped probing when he touched Darvis' mind. He was already thinking that it was a werewolf attack. 'Like we're the only ones that have claws in the world of the supernatural,' thought Brian. Though, he knew after what Darvis had seen last night his obvious thought would be werewolves. After all, he probably didn't want to think about what else could be lurking out there.

He and Ashlee made their way past the officer holding the door and started down the hall where they both could hear that everyone else was waiting. Not to mention the smell of blood that hung to the cops clothing. So much for not messing up the job for forensics.

As soon as they walked through the door of the small interrogation room, Jeff sent everyone out except Darvis and himself.

When everyone was out of ear shot, Jeff spoke. "Thanks for coming in when I know that you guys have other business to attend to tonight." Jeff looked at the two men with horror filled eyes. He may be a cop, but he lived and worked in a small town that nothing ever seemed to happen in. Especially not a murder of this magnitude.

"It's no problem at all Jeff. Rowland and I both told you to seek us out anytime you need help with a freaky case," Brian told Jeff, trying to comfort him with his calming thoughts at the same time. It had been Rowland that suggested that Brian may be able to alter other people's thoughts and emotions if he concentrated hard enough. It worked on humans sometimes, but that was about it. Brian was just thankful that it was working at the time being.

"Where did you guys go after we all got done talking this morning?" Darvis was pacing the small room while he spoke. He smelled of fear and anger and something else Brian couldn't quite pick out. He hadn't smelled this strangeness that morning. He wondered what it could be.

Brian glanced at Ashlee to find that the his eyes had started to glow yellow from the scent that was radiating from Darvis; whether it was the fear or the strange scent Brian himself couldn't identify, he didn't know. Apparently Ashlee's wolf wanted to come out to play. Brian couldn't let him attack Darvis, so he did something he really enjoyed doing to Ashlee. Brian turned and smacked him across the face, sending him flying over the table that was set in the middle of the room and into the wall on the opposite side of the room.

"You two should get out of here." Brian turned yellow eyes of his own on Darvis and Jeff as he stated his warning to them. "Things are about to get a bit hairy in here. Pun not intended."

Darvis was about to protest when Jeff grabbed him by the arm and ushered him out of the room. As they closed the door behind them, they heard something slam into the wall beside the door.

As soon as the door had closed, Ashlee launched himself at Brian with the speed and power of a freight train; slamming him hard enough against the wall to break a hole in the drywall. Before Brian could recover, Ashlee grabbed him by the collar of his shirt and threw him to the ground.

Ashlee, who had begun to change in order to have an advantage in a fight against the more dominant wolf, sank his teeth into Brian's neck. This was a big mistake however. Brian may be hard to piss off, but Ashlee had succeeded in pushing him past his point of anger.

Brian, filled with rage at a lesser wolf besting him even for a second, grabbed the back of Ashlee's head; prying his teeth from his flesh. When he pulled free of Ashlee's death grip on his neck, Brian had a chunk of his own flesh come away from his neck along with Ashlee's teeth.

Once free, Brian took control of the situation by grabbing Ashlee by the wrist and snapping it. Brian was just hoping to get Ashlee calmed down a bit before he would really have to hurt him. 'Leave it to Ash-hole to fuck up a simple talk with the police,' thought Brian as he broke Ashlee's other wrist.

Ashlee rolled off of Brian, clutching his broken hands to his chest. He was too far gone in the change to cry; instead, it came out simply as a whimper.

Brian took advantage of split second that Ashlee nursed his injuries by putting him in a sleeper hold. Though Ashlee struggled, he couldn't break the hold that was cutting off the blood flow to what little brain he had. Brian was thankful for the fact that he was better at hand to hand combat than Ashlee had been. If he had lost, Jeff, Darvis, and the other officers in the station would have been in grave peril. Not to mention

Ashlee would have taken his place in the pack rank. He knew that Ashlee wouldn't remember losing control when he woke up; and that his wrists would be completely healed.

Once unconscious, the changes began to stop and Ashlee regain his full human form. Brian carried Ashlee's limp body out of the room to find a place to lay him down. Jeff and Darvis stared in horror at the man that lie motionless in Brian's arms. "Don't worry guys, I just made him go to sleep for a bit," Brian assured the two police officers. "Though, I don't imagine that he will be in the best of moods when he wakes up. After all, I wouldn't want to wake-up to find I had two broken wrists and no recollection of how it happened."

"What the hell happened in there," asked Darvis. "One second everything seemed fine, and then you sent Ashlee sailing across the room to crash into the far wall."

Jeff glanced at Darvis when he spoke. "You didn't notice how close to losing control Ashlee had gotten. If Brian hadn't been there, you and I would surely be dead. Thank you, Brian."

"It was nothing. In fact, I should be thanking you for giving me the opportunity to smack Ash around some," Brian said with a grin. "Now Rowland can't complain that I hit Ashlee without just cause. If I hadn't, you two would either have died or been changed.

"Though I'm not sure why Ashlee lost control so easily. Hell, I nearly lost it," Brian informed them, turning curious eyes toward Darvis. "It was something about the way you smelled in there. You smelled of anger and fear; plus something I had never scented before. Though, only fear remains on you now. Whatever it was, I felt the urge to kill you because of it. Which is odd since fear usually makes me want to eat a human. This was something strange. I'm glad it is gone. We can worry about what it was later. Now, why do you think that we would be of help in your new case?"

"Like you don't already know the thoughts running through our brains as we speak, Brian." Jeff took a step toward Brian. He was as calm as could be, considering he thought that there was a werewolf that had committed murder in his town. "I know it wasn't you who had done this to the poor woman; or any other of Rowland's wolves for that matter. However, to Darvis and myself, it appears to have been more than a simple animal attack. This woman, Haley Michaels, was killed with claws that no animal I have ever seen in this area had.

"She had been leaving work when she was attacked. She worked at the local Wal-Mart as a sales floor associate. She had been in the parking lot when she was taken. The cart boy had seen her by her car and waved good night to her, and then he went to grab a cart from the lane over.

"That was when he heard the scream a half second later. When he turned around, Haley was gone. She had just vanished.

"She turned up on the opposite end of town not even five minutes from the time she was taken. Her eyes had been clawed out along with her heart."

Brian looked at Jeff and Darvis with intelligent eyes. He was mulling over in his mind what all of this could mean; and how it could be related to the being that had been messing with Rowland's mind. "This wasn't a werewolf, I can promise you that. The kill doesn't fit with the way we kill. Trust me, if it were wolf, there would have been a lot less to identify the body with. Though whatever it was knew that you would blame our kind first. They didn't bank on our working together in the past."

"Thanks Brian. Do you think that Rowland would be able to meet me at the morgue to see what scent he can pick up off the body," Jeff asked. Jeff knew that there was something big going on, but knew better than to ask questions.

"Yeah, let me give him a call," Brian informed Jeff. Then he turned to Darvis, "After Ashlee wakes up, the three of us gotta head out."

"Okay. Should I bring anything with me," Darvis asked Brian. Brian could see images of holy water and crucifixes popping into Darvis' head.

Forcing himself not to laugh out loud, he reached into his jean pocket and retrieved his second pentacle necklace and handed it to Darvis. "Put this on. It will protect you where we are going tonight," Brian told Darvis. "Didn't know how far down the rabbits hole you would be going when you found out the supernatural really existed, did you?"

"Guess not," was all Darvis said before clasping the necklace around his neck. The metal felt warm through his shirt. He almost mentioned that fact, but thought better of it. He didn't know what kind of magic the pendent held, since he was raised that a pentagram was a symbol of evil.

"Actually, the pentacle, not pentagram, is a symbol of good magic. It has been known to protect from evil," Brian informed Darvis.

Darvis glared at Brian. "Could you please not read my thoughts so often? Hasn't anyone told you that it is rude?"

"Huh, never thought about it that way before. It must get annoying having people voice what you are thinking before you get a chance to say it," Brian said pointedly. "But, I'm not changing to sooth other peoples' egos. Reading thoughts has helped me save many lives; including yours a few minutes ago."

"Good point. Well, could you make it a little less obvious?"

"Sure," Brian told Darvis. "But then I couldn't annoy so many people."

Brian reached into his pocket and pulled out his phone. He began dialing Rowland's number without another word to Jeff or Darvis.

The phone rang four times before Rowland finally picked up on the other end, slightly out of breath. "Hey Brian, how could you be done at Candiland already?"

"Rowland, we haven't even made it to Candiland. Ash and I had just gotten to the police station to pick up Darvis when Jeff asked us to come inside." Brian knew that the next part of his conversation with Rowland would upset the other man to a grave extent. "Rowland, there's been a murder. And it wasn't a human doing these killings. Jeff was wondering if you would be so kind as to try to pick up the scent of the killer to help solve the case."

"Sure, tell Jeff that I will meet him at the morgue. Oh, and you guys should be careful. This may be related to whoever is invading my mind."

"I already thought about that. What I don't get is *why* would he kill this woman so violently if he has the power to control minds? He almost cracked your mind and I know how big of a feat that could be," Brian said matter-of-factly. He was trying for humor, but it was lost between him and Rowland due to the seriousness of the situation.

Brian hung up the phone without waiting for a goodbye; and turned back to Jeff and Darvis. "Jeff, Rowland said that he would meet you at the morgue as soon as he can."

"Thanks Brian. I hope things go well with whatever you need Darvis' help with tonight," Jeff said as he put on his jacket. "I will see you boys later. I gotta head out now since I know Rowland will be at the morgue any second. Be careful guys."

Without another word or even to wait for a reply, Jeff walked past Brian and left.

"Darvis, I'm going to need your help to get Ashlee to the truck. I'm thinking that we should handcuff him when we do," Brian told Darvis after Jeff left the building.

"Why would we need to cuff him," asked Darvis.

"Let's just say that cranky werewolves aren't always pleasant to be around."

It took Darvis a second or two to put together what Brian was saying. Brian didn't need telepathy to realize when exactly Darvis figured out just how much danger he could be in trapped in a car with an angry werewolf.

Brian and Darvis went into the other room, where Ashlee slept, to find that Ashlee had already recovered. Brian was surprised at how calm the other man was after their confrontation. 'Maybe Rowland was right about Ash. Maybe there really was hope for him yet,' thought Brian as they entered the room.

Not only was Ashlee conscious, but his hands were completely healed after being nearly crushed by Brian only forty minutes earlier. Even among the wolves that was impressive. 'Apparently Ashlee had a special ability after all. Rapid healing comes in handy, but this was a damn miracle at how quickly he healed himself. Guess that proves that submissive wolves could have gifts after all. Or Ashlee has a greater potential than any of the wolves gave him credit for.'

"How long was I out? And what exactly happened," Ashlee inquired of Brian and Darvis.

Brian sat down beside Ashlee and began filling him in on what had happened while he was out.

After bringing Ashlee up to speed, the three men made their way toward the exit to hop in Brian's truck; and head over to Candiland.

"Next stop Candiland!" Brian was grinning when he said this to Darvis. He could tell just how much it bugged the married man that he was going to a strip club. Of course, Brian didn't mention that this strip club had something for everyone. Meaning it was split between male and female strippers. And he was going to enjoy taking the other guys in through the wrong door. He may not be gay, but male nudity didn't bother him like it does most guys. And he thought that he would surprise Darvis with the fact that it was a supernaturally run and owned facility. After all, this club tended to cater to a select clientele; which was a polite way of saying rich and/or freaky.

"Darvis, you may want to buckle=up. I don't exactly drive fifty-five," Brain said as they pulled out of the parking lot. He and Ashlee both laughed at the scared look on Darvis' face when he looked at the speedometer which already showed they were traveling at around 100 mph.

8: Dead Zone

hen Jeff got to the morgue, he saw Rowland leaning against the side of the building. He had a look of calm on his face, but Jeff knew him well. He could see, even at a distance that, Rowland had been missing sleep by the bags under his eyes. Also, the set of his shoulders said that he was under a lot of stress.

'What could be going on around here that would have Rowland so worked up? I mean, he is after all the most laid back individual I ever met. Even as a human he didn't let much get to him; or he didn't show that it did.'

Jeff broke his train of thought when he pulled his squad car over by the curb in front of the morgue entrance. As he put the vehicle into park, Rowland pushed off the wall and made his way over as Jeff climbed out from behind the wheel.

"So, there has been a murder. You guys think that it is a werewolf. None of your staff wants to blame my wolves. Those that know of our kind that is. Yada yada," Rowland said to Jeff in an annoyed voice that he rarely used toward those he called friend. "So, let's get this over with, shall we. I do have more important things to worry about."

"Okay. Guess it's going to be all business tonight. No 'hey Jeff, how are you today?' I'm so sorry that the dead woman has inconvenienced you," Jeff gave as a mock apology.

"Hey, I'm sorry Jeff. I've been through a lot already today. This so was not on the list of shit I wanted to accomplish when I got up today. Of course, I also didn't want to find out that my mind was being targeted by some unknown being. Then this shit happened. So, I'm a bit cranky." Rowland turned in the middle of his apology and headed toward the door.

Jeff noticed that Rowland's movements were jagged and stiff. He may only have limited knowledge of the way werewolves carried themselves, but he knew enough to realize that the way Rowland was carrying himself was a sign of just how bad things were. Werewolves always walked with a fluid grace that made it appear as if their very bones were bending as they moved.

"Rowland, wait."

"Jeff, I want to get this done," Rowland stated in a calm voice that had the slightest hint of anger to it that Jeff only noticed because of how close he had been with Rowland for years. He knew he was right when Rowland turned to face him. His eyes hadn't turned the yellow they did when he got pissed; but they had turned the ice blue that he had in full wolf form. The eyes were nearly white and were freighting in his human face.

"Down boy," Jeff said to Rowland when he saw the eyes. He wasn't afraid, which he knew was a good thing. If had showed fear, Rowland would have attacked before he had a chance to think of what he was doing.

Rowland shook his head to clear his thoughts. He knew that he had to focus on shielding his mind from the intruder; but with all that was going on he had forgotten, again. Once he felt the presence again, he forced it out. It was getting hard to push the mind that was invading his from his thoughts every time. He knew that he could not afford to let this being in his head again because he wasn't sure he could fight him off anymore.

After Rowland was done battling his inner demon, he realized what Jeff had said. He lost himself in laughter. Whipping tears from his eye, Rowland said, "How many times have I told you, I am not a dog."

"Yeah, sorry 'bout that. I forget since you're such a big softy of a wolf. And you enjoy a game of fetch now and then."

Rowland smiled at his old friend. "Thank you for helping me to realize that this guy, or whatever it is, was taking control of me again. It is getting harder for me to notice when it is happening. I don't know if I will be able to fight him off again. Who knew that your poor sense of humor was what I need to snap me out of it."

"It may be poor humor, but your dumbass laughed at the little joke I made till you were crying," Jeff retorted with false defensiveness. "We can go see the body and see what you think. But after that you have to tell me what's going on with you. You are like a brother to me and I'm worried about you."

Rowland closed the gap between Jeff and himself and put his arms around the other man in a hug that let Jeff know that he thought of him as family as well. "You don't have to worry about me; I will take out whoever it is fucking with me before he has a chance to try his mind games on anyone else. Also, if we were family, you would be more like my father. You are old enough."

"I'm not that much older than you are. Just because you don't age at the rate that humans do; doesn't change how many years that you have lived." Jeff acted as if Rowland's comment had really got to him; but he enjoyed the joking and open criticism that he and Rowland had always had.

Rowland made it to the door first and opened it, waving Jeff to go in before himself. "Age before beauty Jeffy boy."

"Shouldn't you say age before fruity," Jeff replied as he walked through the door ahead of the other man. "And don't stare at my ass as we walk down the hall."

"I will try to refrain from looking at you ass; but that's getting kind of hard when it's growing larger with every year that passes." Both Jeff and Rowland had to stop in the hall to catch their breath after their faux argument because they were laughing so hard.

They walked to the closest stair well and headed down to the basement where the morgue's corpses were located. Rowland had only been down to the morgue one other time since he became a werewolf. It was harder for him than any human could ever imagine going down there. It smelled of death and meat.

Rowland's mouth started water as soon as they reached the basement landing. He didn't mention this to Jeff. He knew that Jeff would only compare him to Pavlov's dog.

Instantly he smelled something out of place. He knew without a doubt that this was the creature he was supposed to identify. Yet it wasn't just one scent that he noticed that was out of place. Yeah, all of the scents were from the same kind of creature, but there were maybe five different ones.

When he entered the room he got a better whiff of the things. He could tell that there had definitely been five of these creatures attacking the woman that lie on the table in the middle of the room. She apparently was having her autopsy as soon as Rowland finished his examination.

"Jeff, I hate to give you bad news, but I have never scented one of whatever kind of creature this is before. The only thing I can say for sure is that they have feathers, like on wings perhaps. Though whether it's a feature they have all of the time or a shifted thing like with us wolves, I don't know," Rowland told Jeff with pain in his voice.

Rowland had always been a bit of a pacifist by nature and becoming a werewolf had not changed that much. Seeing the woman on the table like this, Jeff knew, caused Rowland more pain than any physical blow could ever cause him. How such a gentle man could strike fear into the hearts of most of the supernatural community baffled Jeff.

"Well, now we know that it was a group of assailants. And we can rule out rogue wolves. Also, we think that the heart and eyes missing are related to some ritual occult shit," Jeff informed Rowland. Jeff didn't want to have Rowland feeling like he had let him down.

"I have to call Brain and let him know what we have discovered. Maybe Marzipan will know something of these creatures that would help us. Then I will fill you in on the shit that has gone down today. Including how well Rudi is doing already. Then, after Brian, Ashlee, and Darvis get whatever info they can, you and I can head to the place where the body was found to see if I can pick up the scent," Rowland reached into his pocket and grabbed his phone. He turned toward the door as he dialed Brian's number.

"Brian, we still don't know what attacked that poor woman. However, I do know that there were five of these creatures doing the killing," Rowland told Brian before he could even say a word. "These things may fly and they smell of feathers. Possibly a type of bird demon that I have not yet come across. Ask Marzipan about this also." Without saying goodbye, Rowland hung up the phone and climbed into the passenger seat of Jeff's squad car.

"Come on old man," Rowland called out of the window at Jeff.

Shaking his head, Jeff made his way out of the morgue; and climbed into the driver's seat and buckled his seatbelt. "So, what the hell is going on in this town?"

"That's a good question, but I don't have an answer for it. Not yet anyway." Rowland turned to look out the window.

He was lost in thought for a moment, thinking of where to begin with his tale of what had happened earlier during the pack meeting. Finally, he turned back to Jeff and started to fill the other man in on what had been transpiring.

9: Candiland

rian put down his phone and filled Darvis in on what Rowland had said. "So, you're saying that we have multiple problems with supernatural forces in our small town; and your pack is our only hope to stop it," Darvis asked

"We aren't the only hope," Ashlee chimed from the backseat. "We could call on the fairies and wood nymphs to help."

"Really," Darvis asked.

Ashlee burst out laughing and said, "The only fairy we know is our alpha."

With speed fast enough that the truck didn't even swerve, Brian turned around and punched Ashlee between the eyes, breaking his nose.

"Don't be so disrespectful Ash-hole. Plus, wood nymphs and fairies are real. Nymphs are really nice, I met a few when I was trying to find where I belonged after I was turned. Though, I have never met a fairy that I really cared for, those tricky little fucks. Always stealing shit that doesn't belong to them; then trying to get something in exchange for that item being returned," Brian informed the other two men in the car.

"Wow, I wonder what other creatures really exist," Darvis said to himself.

Brian glanced over at Darvis with a look in his eyes that said he really didn't want to know what horrors lurked out there. It was bad enough that he was about to be introduced to a demon and a few other creatures that go bump in the night once they got to Candiland.

"So, are we there yet," Ashlee asked from the backseat, smirking at Brian in the rearview mirror. His nose had almost healed; along with the two black eyes that any human would have gotten from having their nose broken.

"Why are you always so childish?"

"It's a blessing. I'm like a freakin Toy'r'us kid."

Brian just rolled his eyes at Ashlee's comment. He had to force himself not to laugh though. 'Don't want to give the guy incentive to really never grow-up,' Brian thought as he stifled his own smile. He just glared at Ashlee in the mirror, giving him cold, emotionless eyes.

Of course this would have worked at getting Ashlee to act his age if Darvis hadn't been giggling like a school girl at him. Yes, that's right, he was honest to God giggling. That was all Brian could take of trying to not laugh at the immaturity that Ashlee displayed. Brian laughed with his booming bark like laughter along with the other men till he was having trouble catching his breath.

"Seriously, where do you come up with this shit? Do you find little kids and still their material," Brian inquired, trying to regain his stand at not finding humor in Ashlee's comments. But he was failing miserably. He would never admit it out load, but Ashlee wasn't such a bad guy when you got to hangout with him a bit. Getting to hit him and break bones knowing that he would heal within minutes helped more than Ashlee's personality.

"How about you turn on some jams, Brian? You are always talkin about how much better your system is than everyone we know. Let's see what all you're talking about," Ashlee said. He really could care less what Brian's stereo system was like, but he was growing tired of feeling like he had to come up with dumb comments to fill their time while they were stuck in the vehicle.

"You do realize I could hear everything that you were just thinking," Brian reminded Ashlee who shied away a bit, clearly not wanting to be hit again. "But you got a point, music would be nicer than listening to you talk the rest of the trip."

"Darvis, what type of music would you like to listen to," Brian asked his passenger. "I'm not picky and I really don't care if it annoys Ashlee. In fact, it would make me more than happen to have him annoyed." Brian looked into the mirror to see Ashlee give him the finger.

Brian, keeping his cool as usual, just smiled back at Ashlee. 'Really dude, I like women. You can stop making offers at me like that,' Brian projected into Ashlee's mind.

Ashlee just crossed his arms over his chest and turned his head to stare out the window. He had never taken well to criticism. Brian felt bad when he glanced back at the lesser wolf in the backseat. He thought at Ashlee, 'Man, I'm sorry if I offended you. I know for a fact that you're straight. Remember, I know what you think about all too often. Gay guys tend to think about other reproductive organs. Imagine the things I have heard and seen in Rowland's mind. And you wonder why I'm so okay with the gay stuff.'

'Thanks Brian. I just get tired of people always thinking that I'm a fag, you know. I have nothing against gay people, really. Hell, one of my best friends is gay. Granted he isn't exactly a stereotype. Not that there *is* a freakishly powerful gay werewolf stereotype. However, it would be nice to not catch shit for hanging with him. Rowland's one of the greatest friends I could ever ask for.' Ashlee furrowed his brow as he thought this toward Brian, almost as if he were fighting back tears.

'Trust me, I understand what you mean. People used to call me gay and shit before I joined the military. Hell some of them thought that I only joined to try to quash those rumors that I was gay. Now that my mind reading has been supercharged by becoming a werewolf, the gay thing isn't a problem that I worry about. Everything will work out in due time, you will see.'

'You mean like you and Kristie?' Ashlee arched one of his eyebrows at the look on Brian's face when he thought this at him. Ashlee could tell that he was sure that he hadn't shown any sign that he may harbor feelings toward Kristie.

'I have no idea what you are talking about.'

'That's bullshit and you know it. I have seen how you look at her. You like her as more than just a friend. You want her as your mate. And trust me, she wants you too. How could you not know that?'

'She has a natural defense against my power to read minds. She isn't the only one either. Stephen has the same ability as well and he's only human.' Brian felt hope for the first time since he noticed that he had feelings for Kristie.

'Well that makes sense why you haven't made your move yet. When you see her next, grab her and kiss her. She will love that.' Ashlee was enjoying playing matchmaker. He had very good skills when women were concerned. He wasn't the slut that he once had been, but he still could pull a lot of game if he wished. He was just tired of being that guy and wanted to settle down with a good girl and start a family. Only problem was finding the girl to do so with.

'Yeah, maybe I will do that.' Brian had never been that forward with the girls and knew himself well enough that he would ask her for a date instead of forcing himself on Kristie.

Though Brian and Ashlee had had a big heart to heart, less than a minute had passed during their mental conversation. The speed of thought was a great way to talk.

Brian had almost forgotten that he had asked Darvis a question until the other man answered it. "I like anything other than country. I really don't like that 'tear in your beer' shit. I prefer rock, but rap and stuff's cool by me. Just put anything on."

Brian turned the radio on to one of the local rock stations and cranked up the volume, ending all conversation for the duration of their trip.

They pulled into the parking lot at Candiland around eleven thirty.

It was a Sunday, yet the parking lot was reasonably full, considering that everyone would need to get up for work the next morning. It took Brian nearly ten minutes to finally find a spot that his truck would fit in.

He put the truck into park and started climbing out of the cab, after killing the engine. The three men walked side by side in silence on their way up to the building with the huge neon sign reading 'Candiland.' The name on the sign looked like large candy canes, with its red and white strips. The front door even had a doorknob that looked like a gumdrop.

"Okay, if some old lady tries to fatten me up when I get inside, I'm outta here," Ashlee said as he noticed the very Hansel and Gretel look to the front of the building.

"Old ladies are going to be the least of your problems inside here," Brian assured Ashlee. "Demons and other supernatural creatures are far worse than grandmas."

"You never met my grandma," Ashlee said under his breath so low that Darvis hadn't heard. However, Brian snorted with laughter when Ashlee said this about his own grandmother.

As they reached the door, Brian grabbed the gumdrop knob. "Shall we get this over with," he asked the other two guys before opening the door. Darvis and Ashlee both nodded to the affirmative and they proceeded into the club.

Once inside the door, the lady working the front desk greeted them. "Welcome to 'Candiland,' I am Lollipop. We have entertainment for all walks of life here. The club is divided into two halves. On the left we have the male entertainers; and on the right we have the female entertainers. What would you prefer?"

Before Ashlee could blurt out female, Brian shoved his way to the desk around the gawking Ashlee. Ashlee apparently had never seen a banshee before. He probable thought that she would be a wailing hag. Well, the wailing part was accurate when they are provoked. Though, the banshee usually did their wailing to announce that death was about to take a member of a royal blood line.

"Actually, we are here on business," Brian informed Lollipop. She looked at him for the first time and her eyes got wide.

"Brian! I didn't know that you were going to grace us with you presence this evening," Lollipop told him. "Follow me. I will take you to Marzipan." Lollipop turned to a gentleman behind the counter. "Hey Francisco, I'm going to take the wolves to see our mistress. Watch the counter."

Francisco followed the order without complaint. Considering Francisco was an animated corps, he still looked good. 'Obviously Marzipan had a powerful necromancer on her payroll,' Brian noted mentally. Know thy enemy like you know yourself had always been Brian's motto. Having that type of mind set has saved him from being the one in the body bag a few times.

They made their way through a door that read "Employees only." The door led them to a hall lined with other doors that were marked as restrooms, male and female dressing rooms, and at the very end of the hall was a door that a vibrant orange with a golden name plate that read "Marzipan's Office: Owner/Performer" in diamonds.

"Damn!" Ashlee let out a low whistle at the sight of the stones used to spell out the message on the name plate. "This bitch must be rollin in the dough."

Lollipop turned as Ashlee spoke. Her eyes, which are usually a pale grey, had turn blood red with fury. Her well manicured nails grew into talons as she crouched in a feral posture, like a cat getting ready to pounce. She was focused entirely on Ashlee as she opened her mouth and filled her lungs with air.

Brian saw in her mind what she was about to do. He had heard how devastating the wail of a banshee could be; and when he viewed Lollipop's intent, he knew how understated her and her kin's abilities had really been.

Before Lollipop could release the scream that was building in her throat, Brian was behind her with his hand over her mouth. 'Calm down Lollipop. You don't want to do this. If you attack my pack brother, no matter how much I despise him, I would have no choice but to attack you in retaliation,' Brian warned the woman that was struggling in his arms.

Lollipop stopped trying to break free and just relaxed in Brian's arms. 'Thank you. I just lose my head when people talk bad about my mistress. I'm so embarrassed that you had to witness that Brian. What you must think of me and my kind now.'

"Don't worry about it," Brian said aloud. "No harm no foul."

"I am so sorry that I lost control. It seems to be happening to a lot of us lately," Lollipop informed Brian and the others. "Sometimes I'm myself; then, a moment later, I'm on edge and about to rip the head off somebody. It's like someone's trying to control me. Sometimes I swear that I can hear a whisper in my mind telling me to do things."

Brian looked at the woman as if he was seeing her for the first time. 'That's exactly what has been happening to our alpha. We need to see if Marzipan knows what could be doing this. It appears that our pack isn't the only ones being targeted by this unknown being.' This new information bothered Brian. It would seem that the entire preternatural community was under attack.

"May we please go in and speak to Marzipan now. My wife was already mad when I told her that I had to help with a case and was going to be working a lot of over time. She is one person no one wants to make mad," Darvis said to Lollipop.

"Sure thing sweetie," Lollipop said; and turned toward the door. She reached for the handle and hesitated. "I hope that Marzipan isn't being targeted by this stranger that is messing with my mind also. An alpha wolf and a banshee would be nothing compared to a demon under the control of whatever this thing is. She can be quit deadly by herself; I'd hate to be in her way if someone else was in the driver's seat of her mind."

Brian knew that she was right. He also knew that, like him, she could tell if someone was prying around in her mind. This person would have to be pretty powerful to get in her mind and take over. Marzipan was stubborn, strong willed, and could be downright cold when she wanted to be.

Lollipop turned the knob and pushed the door open after she was sure that she had composed herself enough to not alarm Marzipan with what had just happened. She stepped through the doorway and waved the three men inside. "Please, take a seat and I will go let Marzipan know that you have arrived," Lollipop told them while indicating three chairs that had been brought into the office for their meeting. The chairs were sitting in front of a very expensive looking wooden desk that had a dark Brazilian walnut finish. Each of the chairs were old high back chairs. Even the one behind the desk was a high back chair of the same finish as the desk. Its cushion was thick with padding and upholstered with a silky fabric that looked like it was made in ancient times, which was likely with Marzipan.

"You really don't have to go find her," Brian assured Lollipop. "I told her we were here already. In fact, she in the hall right now."

10: Demon-stration of Kindness

second later a woman appeared in the doorway. Marzipan was a little over five feet in height. She had long, straight black hair that was accented with a head dress that was nearly as ancient as she was herself. She looked like an Egyptian Pharaoh, which was a very good possibility that she had been one.

"Wow," Ashlee exclaimed when Marzipan entered the room. "You look like Cleopatra. Is that what you are going for during your performance?"

"Of course not," Marzipan explain with a very seductive purr to her accented voice. "I am the one that was once called Cleopatra. I now go by the name Marzipan because I wouldn't want those pathetic humans to realize I am still around."

"Hello," Darvis spoke up. "Mixed company. I am human. I'd appreciate not being spoken about like I'm not standing right here."

Marzipan looked at Darvis with a suspicious glint in her eyes. "Of course, I am terribly sorry. I just sensed that you may not be entirely human. There is a power that seems to be radiating from you. But that it is obvious now that I was wrong. It must be coming from a powerful amulet of sorts." Marzipan turned to face Brian at that moment. "You have done you research, my sweet. Would you not like to continue what we started last time you were here? Rowland is not here to stop us this time."

As she spoke, she made her way over to Brian. When she reached his side, she rubbed her hand tentatively down the side of his face.

Brian jumped back from her touch as if it had burned his flesh. His eyes blazed yellow as he growled a warning to Marzipan to stay back.

"Oh, you make me sad Brian. I was hoping that you missed me as much as I have missed you. You were the first guy in over a century that got away before I had finished feeding. The others had always come back begging for me to feed from them again. Yet, you deny me even another taste," Marzipan told Brian. She seemed genuinely upset by the fact that someone was able to resist her. Well, someone that wasn't into men anyway.

"Brian, you should really take that necklace of yours off. We could have lots of fun if we shared her," Ashlee told Brian, though he couldn't seem to peal his eyes away from Marzipan's radiant face.

When Ashlee made his comment, Marzipan turned from Brian with a sly smile spreading across her face. "I'm shocked that Brian brought you in to see me without an amulet of your own. What is your name?"

"You can call me Ash."

"So Ash, would you like to join me for dinner after Brian gets done questioning me about this new power that has come to our area of the world," Marzipan purred to Ashlee.

Ashlee closed his eyes and moaned with pleasure at just hearing this temptress's voice. 'If her voice can do that to me, what else could she do?'

"How did you know what we had come to talk to you about? I didn't feel you invading my mind for information," Brian asked of Marzipan.

Marzipan smiled sweetly and replied, "One doesn't survive as long as I have without keeping a weather eye out for large powers invading their territory."

"As much as I would enjoy watching you feed on Ashlee..." Brian began until Ashlee interrupted

"I knew you would want to watch me hooking up with a chick. Man, you are really sick," Ashlee said.

Brian reached back and smacked Ashlee upside the head. "As I was saying, I'd like to see Ashlee getting his just desserts. However, Rowland wants us to report to him as soon as we get some information from you."

"You always try to spoil my fun. Try being to opportune word," Marzipan said to Brian.

Before anyone could blink, Marzipan had thrown herself into Ashlee, sending the both of them sailing over the desk to land on the floor behind it. When they had landed, Ashlee looked up at Marzipan expecting to see the same beautiful woman that had propositioned him moments earlier. However, the thing that straddled him was anything but beautiful.

Marzipans nails had grown into four inch talons that were dripping with some strange liquid that smelled a bit rancid. Her beautiful honey brown eyes had turned black. Even the white parts of her eyes had been taken over completely by the blackness that seemed as though there was no end to it. When she opened her mouth, her tongue looked serpentine; the end of it had an opening with little barbs on it. Her teeth had grown into sharp points like those of a piranha.

After Marzipan's glamour was dropped, Ashlee no longer wanted to be this close to her. Hell, he didn't even want to be in the same city as this thing.

Ashlee tried to back away, but Marzipan was too quick for him. She bent down and put her arms around Ashlee's back. When she had him in her arms, she pressed her talons through his shirt and into his skin on either side of his spine.

Almost instantly after the talons punctured the skin, Ashlee stopped struggling. All his fear of what Marzipan had turned into was gone. He saw the beautiful woman again. He had no desire to run away now. In fact, Marzipan was the single thing that really seemed to matter anymore.

Marzipan bent over as if to kiss him and Ashlee felt what should have been a tongue sliding down his throat. Ashlee began to panic when he felt this. That was when he realized that he couldn't move a muscle at all. He could still feel pain, but it was pleasuring. If it hadn't been for the snake tongue slithering through him, he would have been enjoying the experience.

Then, without warning, Marzipan sprang back from Ashlee with a look of terror in her eyes.

Brian was less than a foot away from the succubus when she had sprang away from his pack brother. He clearly had intended to rescue Ashlee from such a terrible fate that goes along with being snacked on by a succubus. He knew that a sort of infatuation was inevitable in most cases involving a succubus' neurotoxins that are secreted from pores at the base of its talons. He still remembered the time that he had been put under Marzipan's 'spell;' and the feeling of helplessness that he felt when she came around him even to this day.

The look of shock on Brian's face told Ashlee that he hadn't been the one to save him. Then, rolling his eyes to look above his head because his body still wouldn't respond to him, he observed Darvis standing there with a smoking gun in his clutches. He was shaking with fear and anger. Ashlee was glad that he couldn't use his senses at the moment; he didn't want to lose control again tonight because some poor excuse for a cop couldn't control his own emotions.

Brian, realizing that his back was turned to the very angry demon, turned to find that she had turned back into the beautiful façade that she showed the world. Besides the bullet hole in her right shoulder, she appeared intact.

"What the hell did you do that for," Marzipan spat at Darvis. Her temper was clearly not in check as she spoke to the cop that had just shot her. "What are you?"

"I'm a police officer from Albany," Darvis answered in a shaky voice. "Stay where you are or I will shoot again."

"Like that thing could kill me." As she spoke, her wound had already closed up completely before their eyes. All that remained was a tiny bruise. Then a second later, even that little sign of the bullet hole was gone. "Clearly you didn't pay attention to the lack of security in my club. I don't have to worry about being taken down by the weapons of man."

Darvis could hardly believe his eyes. Just the night before he would have thought that something like this was impossible. Now his eyes seemed to have been ripped wide open to the world of the supernatural. The things that we instinctively fear were real and he had just pissed one of them off. 'Just my luck; I pick something I can't kill or defend myself from to make enemies with,' Darvis thought as he lowered his gun.

"Oh, you don't need to fear me, human. I have acquired a taste for supernatural beings. Humans are less to feed on because of how simple their minds have become; not to mention how quickly they die. Not very appetizing if you ask me," Marzipan told Darvis in a manner that was intended to be reassuring. However, all she seemed to be doing was reassuring him that she wouldn't enjoy 'loving' him to death as much as she would have another person that was of a more powerful delight.

"Gee, I'm so glad that I would be a burden on you if you decided to make a snack out of me," Darvis replied to Marzipan with a mock grin spreading on his face.

"Okay. Could we just get down to business? We have other matters to attend to after we get the information that we need from you, Marzipan," Brian said, stepping between the angry demon and the police officer that were still squaring off. "Can we, please, sit down and talk so that we can be on our way?"

"Absolutely. I was only teasing the little human," Marzipan informed Brian with a tone that said clearly how much she thought of herself as being above all other beings. "Besides, that other wolf wasn't very tasty. Not after having a taste of a more powerful wolf."

"HELLO! I am still here," Ashlee chimed in as he began to pull himself to his feet. He was still pale from the neurotoxin that had been coursing through his veins. Yet he was moving and speaking already.

"Wow! How are you even moving, let alone speaking, after I had my talons buried inside of you," Marzipan inquired of the man that she had just deemed a lesser wolf; and unworthy of being a snack. "Maybe you are a bit more powerful than I had originally thought. Guess you just taste bad."

"Thanks, bitch. And you weren't exactly a treat yourself," Ashlee retorted with malice in his voice. He clearly didn't like being told that he was bad by a sex demon. "I have banged fat bitches that had better skills when it came to sex than you. Of course, they hadn't been trying to kill me."

"Ashlee, shut up. We need to get this over with and you're wasting time," Brian said to his pack brother. He wasn't intending to be obviously threatening toward Ashlee after the guy just had his ass handed to him by a woman. Granted that woman could bench press a fully loaded semi, it was still emasculating. However, he couldn't keep the hint of a growl out of the tone in which he used. Being on edge was really beginning to get to him; and Brian wanted nothing more than to finish up with Marzipan. Then he could help Rowland with the murder case. And, if he was lucky, he could actually make it home at a decent time for a change. He knew that things were going to get worse before they got better around the town of Albany. He also knew that he was going to need all his strength if his pack would stand a chance against another telepath, especially one that Brian knew without meeting was far more powerful than he was. 'Guess I'm going to need to get my psychic work-outs more regular if I want to stand a chance against this foe.'

"Sorry, Brian," Ashlee said with sincerity, which took Brian by surprise. He didn't even think that Ashlee was capable of a genuine apology. ##Ashlee was shaken by the experience; but didn't want anyone to know how much fear he felt for the demon that was still only a few paces away from him. Brian may not be close to Ash outside of pack business, but he could see fear in Ashlee's eyes. Not to mention the smell of it that was seeping off of him like a rancid cologne. And the fact that he could read his thoughts; which were screaming to get this over with so that he could get away from Marzipan.

"It's fine. Just take a seat and we can get this talk over with," Brian told Ashlee, keeping sympathy out of his voice. Though, he did project it to him via his mind.

Brian was surprised when they walked around to take their seats that Darvis signaled to Ashlee to take the middle seat. It was almost like he had read Brian's mind and knew that Ashlee would feel safer in the middle of the two of them.

They waited for Marzipan to take her seat before they took their own. "Glad to see that chivalry isn't dead after all," Marzipan stated, clearly pleased that the guys were acting like gentlemen after the events that had just transpired. "Now, what would you like to ask me? I promise that I will help you in any way I can."

"Well, there are two things that we need to talk about with you," Brian began. "First, Rowland has been having a bit of a problem controlling his temper lately. At first we just chalked it up as a bad mood, which Rowland is in more often than most people think. Gay guys tend to be very moody. But this was different. Normally when Rowland is in a pissy mood, he represses it so that nobody would ever know. I only know because of my ability to read thoughts. It wasn't until a few hours ago that we realized it was more than just mood swings. I noticed a presence in his mind that shouldn't be there. As soon as Rowland and I found the invading persons thoughts, we were able to force him out. By we, I mean Rowland himself forced the invader out. Rowland is in danger of being taken over if he lets his defenses slip even a little bit."

"That would be very problematic. Rowland may not seem like it, but he is by far the most powerful werewolf that I have ever come across. His gentle nature is the only thing that keeps his true potential from showing. If this person, or whatever, is strong enough to effect him, then the whole supernatural community could be in grave danger," Marzipan said out load, though it was clear that she was talking to herself.

"That's not all," Brian continued. "Since we have been here, we discovered that our pack isn't all that this being is after. He has been terrorizing at least one member of your staff. Lollipop nearly attacked us before we even got inside of you office. I found the same presence in her mind and forced it out. What could possibly be doing this to such powerful beings?"

"I have come across something like this before; while I was ruling over Egypt," Marzipan said, this time actually addressing the men on the opposite side of her desk. "It is a type of sorcery that is very rare; and can be very dangerous in the wrong hands. Though, back than it was only effective on humans. This person, and yes it is a human, has got to be the most powerful mage that the world has seen in a few thousand years. And this magic is very dark. I fear that mind control may be the least of our worries."

"What do you mean by that," Ashlee asked, managing to keep the shakiness out of his voice completely as he addressed his attacker.

"Well, my sweet, we have no idea if our fair community is the first that this person has tried to control. For all we know, he could have an army at his disposal already," Marzipan explained as if to a small child.

"Ok, so we will worry about that when we know more," Brian interjected before Ashlee lost control of his smart mouth. "The second thing that we wanted to talk with you about was a murder that had happened earlier tonight. Darvis, could you show her the pictures of the victim please?"

"Um, I don't have authorization to show these photos to civilians," Darvis told Brian, glancing at the man with nervous eyes.

"We need her help Darvis. She may know what we are dealing with by the carnage in the photograph. It could really help the case," Brian said. Darvis could tell that he was trying to appeal to his better nature as a police officer. And it was working.

Darvis reached into his jacket pocket and pulled out an envelope that read evidence on the front of it. He sat the envelope down on the desk and slid it to the other side, avoiding the reach of the demon on the opposite side of the desk.

Marzipan scooped up the evidence with eager hands and rapidly opened the envelope. She just stared at the pictures, one after another, until she had seen them all. Finally, after a moment of thought, she spoke. "Clearly, whatever had done this had killed the woman because she had gotten in the way of whatever business they were previously engaged in."

"How can you tell that from the photographs that you just looked at," Darvis asked.

"It's simple. The way the eyes were ripped out represents the fact that she had seen something she shouldn't have. Then you have the other damage. It is so violent that it surely is a warning to others not to mettle in the affairs of these creatures."

"What could have done this," Brian questioned.

"Well, that's the problem," Marzipan began. "There are so many creatures that are capable of doing this kind of damage that it is hard to say. Even a human could do this if they were pushed to it. Unless, you have a little more information in which you would care to share." Marzipan was staring straight into Brian's eyes when she said the last bit. He shivered at the cold stare, feeling her boring into his very soul.

"Well, Rowland went to the morgue to try to get a scent for what had killed the woman. He had never come across the scent of these creatures before, so we are still in the dark," Brian filled Marzipan in on what he and Rowland had discussed before he had made it to Candiland.

Marzipan folded her hands in front of her as she thought. "I have heard of a few creatures that could sprout wings at will. But there are only two creatures that can sprout wings that also would have the talons required to cause the damage that had been done to your victim. Those would be Harpies and Sirens. Both of them nasty creatures, and are cousins to one another. The only difference is that a Siren can sing people to their death by getting them to 'fall in love' with them. It only affects men..."

"Why is it that men are always the ones affected when it comes to most spells," Ashlee asked, cutting Marzipan's explanation short.

"Because, my simple minded snack, men are weak. Where was I? Oh, it only affects men and grants the Siren complete control over them by stripping away their will power. The only bad thing is that no one has seen Sirens or Harpies for over a thousand years. I had thought that they were extinct. I hope that, if this is either of these creatures, they aren't aligned with the mage in the area. Also, Sirens and Harpies travel in groups. That's all the information I have for you. Can I get back to running my club? After all, I'm starving." As she spoke, Marzipan stood and headed toward the door.

The three men got out of their seats and slowly made their way toward the door. None of the guys were thrilled that they had to pass by Marzipan at such close proximity. However, none of the guys would let their fear of being grabbed keep them from leaving.

Brian brought up the back of their little group as they passed through the threshold of Marzipans office and back into the long hallway that led to the main area where the entertainment was sure to be going on.

While they were walking down the hall, two people stepped into the hall from one of the dressing rooms. 'It's a bit odd that a male and a female came out of a dressing room together,' thought Brian as they continued down the hall toward the new comers.

When they got closer, Brian could see that the dressing room the two performers had exited from was one of the VIP dressing room that Marzipan had set-up for her favorite strippers. It was the dressing room held for Kit and Kat, the twin werecat sensation that had been drawing audiences for some time now.

As they neared the twin cats, Ashlee stopped in his tracks. Instinct took over and he went into an attack stance/crouch. His lips pealed back to show his teeth. As he snarled, his teeth started turning from human to canine. His eyes skipped the glowing amber yellow that accompanied the change during a loss of control and went straight to the soft brown of his wolf. When the instinct took hold, there isn't any reasoning with a wolf till after the change is done. And the only way to reason with the wolf was to attack him.

"Shit," Brian swore. "I so didn't need this tonight. Marzipan, get Kit and Kat out of here!"

#"What's going on?" Marzipan was approaching with wrath in her step after being ordered to do something by a lesser being. She calmed instantly as Ashlee growl reverberated off the walls of the cramped hallway. "Oh, I see. Kit! Kat! Get out of here! There is a werewolf about to loss himself to instinct in the building. Take the rest of the night off."

"Darvis," Brian yelled at the police officer that was reaching for his gun. "You know that thing isn't going to help the situation. Here!" Brian tossed the keys to his truck to Darvis, who fumbled with them but didn't drop them. "Get the truck and pull up to the doors. I'm goin to try to take Ashlee out before he changes completely."

"Good idea," replied Darvis while he turned and headed for the exit.

Brian turned back toward Ashlee with a smirk of anticipation spreading across his face. "Three times in one night I get to kick your ass. And I didn't think that my night could get any better."

Ashlee, still consumed by the instinct to change and kill the cats, paid no attention to Brian as he approach. The only thoughts running through his mind were those of carnage and death. He didn't even flinch as his bones began to break and reform as the transformation progressed into the next stage.

Brian began to slowly move around behind Ashlee in order to flank him and have a better chance of putting him in a sleeper hold. However, as he got to Ashlee's side, Ashlee let out a blood curdling howl that froze Brian in his tracks for an instant. Brian knew then that the chock hold would never work at this point of the transformation. He was too late to execute his original plan.

He looked around the narrow hallway for another plan to form in his rapidly processing mind. His gaze fell on the dressing room that Kit and Kat had come out of. He snapped his fingers and bolted through the dressing room door. He knew that at this point, Ashlee would follow the scent of the two werecats almost anywhere. He grabbed the first article of clothing that he could find that had a strong scent left on it. 'Good thing cats like to rub their scent on their belongings so much,' Brian thought as he exited the dressing room and went back into the abandoned hallway.

"SHIT," Brian exclaimed when he noticed that Ashlee was no longer in the hall. "Rowland isn't going to be happy about this."

Brian went to the spot where he had last seen Ashlee in order to pick up his scent trail. As he inhaled through his nose, he heard a growl coming from the main entrance. He knew instantaneously that the growl had been that of Ashlee. He didn't sound angry or aggressive. On the contrary, he sounded confused and scared.

Brian was out of the hall and into the lobby before he could even blink. No one, not even the huge wolf that was surrounded by bouncers that were trying to contain the beast, noticed as Brian burst into the room.

It didn't take Ashlee long to notice Brian, for Brian's energy was pulsating from him in hot waves that helped sooth Ashlee's wolf. Ashlee turned to face the more dominate wolf with worried eyes. 'Brian, what's going on? I don't remember changing.'

'It's alright. Just slowly make you way to me and we can get out of here. I will explain everything to you on our way back to town,' Brian projected at the wolf.

Ashlee sank low to the ground as he crawled through the bouncers. One of the bouncers reached out to try and grab Ashlee as he made his escape; but Brian grabbed his hand before he had it extended. "That would not be a smart thing to do," Brian told the bouncer with an authoritative edge to his voice. Though, it was probably the glowing eyes and the growl that followed the command that had the bouncer frozen in fear, not the command itself.

The bouncer jerked his hand away from Brian as though he had been burned; and he backed away slowly.

"Come on Ash. Let's get a move on so that we may get a little sleep tonight," Brian commanded the wolf that was cowering behind him. An on looker may have found humor in the way the monstrous beast cowered and shook like a scared puppy. However, Brian didn't see in humor in it himself. Mostly he felt pity that something like this had happened to his pack brother. Most werewolves would have been more fierce; but Rowland's pack was to caring to harm other humans. Unless they had to of course.

They were out the door and into the truck that sat idling just outside before anyone else could say a word, or try to stop them.

"Ashlee, get off my lap," Brian screamed at the oversized wolf that seemed to think that he was a lap dog.

Ashlee licked the side of Brian's face before Brian could throw him into the backseat. 'Thanks for looking out for me,' the wolf projected at Brian.

Brian hefted Ashlee over the seat and into the back. 'Don't mention it. This doesn't make us friends though; I was under orders from Rowland to keep you alive tonight. I was just doing my job,' Brian said to Ashlee.

Though, it was more than just his duty to the pack and his alpha that kept him from abandoning Ashlee. He knew all to well how things could happen when one lost control of their beast. 'Also, you kiss me in any form again and you will regret it. That's a promise.'

Ashlee just stared Brian in the eyes as he spoke to him via mind. He wasn't making eye contact in a challenging way, which other wolves would have mistaken it for. Rather, he was just listening intently to what Brian was telling him. Brian normally would have been offended by the stare down. However, he was glad that Ashlee was listening for a change. That was until the kissing part of the conversation when Ashlee let a sly, toothy grin spread across his wolf face. 'You know you liked it,' Ashlee teased as he sprawled out to nap in the backseat.

"Darvis, we gotta get back to fill Rowland and Jeff in on what we have discovered tonight. Get us there fast," Brian ordered.

"Sure thing," Darvis confirmed as he slammed his foot down on the gas peddle and the truck leapt forward.

11: The Missing

owland jumped as his phone started vibrating. He had been lost in his own train of thought, and not paying attention to what Jeff had been talking to him about. It wasn't till his phone went off that he even remembered being with Jeff.

Glancing over at the police chief, Rowland noticed that he appeared wearier than he had ever seen him. 'Wonder what it is about this case that has him so worried? When Brian gets here I may have to make him probe Jeff's mind to see what's really bothering him.'

Rowland flipped open his phone and pressed the answer key. "Brian, how did things go?"

"Well, they went as well as to be expected. Marzipan was pleasant as always. Though, we did have a few problems," Brian said in a mild voice to try to assure his Alpha that everything was alright.

"What do you mean you had problems," Rowland demanded of his second without using his Alpha Call. He could tell by how forced the calm in Brian's voice seemed to be that the 'few problems' part was a bit of an understatement. It didn't take super wolf hearing to know that the story would be more extensive than Brian let on at the time being.

Even without the added bonus of the call, Rowland request for information sent shivers down Brian's spin. However, Brian wasn't about to discuss this over the phone, so he ground his teeth to fight the urge to be a loyal wolf. His only reply was, "It's a long story. One such story in which should be discussed in person, not over the phone. I will see you soon."

Rowland didn't have time to agree before the phone went dead. He worried that they may not have had a successful mission. Though, it appeared that all of them must be still in one piece. He may not know what resides in Brian's head like Brian does with others; but he did trust that he wouldn't keep something like that from him. He trusted Brian with his life and was sure he had a very good reason not to reveal information over the phone. 'Of course, Brian could get a bit paranoid at times. Though, who could blame him after what he had been through.'

"So, where are they going to meet us," Jeff asked. He apparently had been listening in on Rowland's conversation and had realized that there was no mention of a rendezvous point.

"Brian will contact you with his mind when they get to town," Rowland told Jeff. "Let's go check out that crime scene and see if I can't find a trail for us to follow."

"Alright, we are only a few minutes away from the scene right now. We should have time for you to look it over before the others even hit town."

"Good," Rowland confirmed. "And Jeff, I know that you aren't telling me everything about this case, but you really shouldn't keep things from me if you want me to help."

"I'm sorry Rowland, but there are some things that I can't share with you and your pack. It's nothing personal, it's just not related to the case that I am having you help with."

"Jeff, are you sure that it isn't related? I mean, hell, we don't even know what we are up against. For all you know, whatever is going on around here could be what you are looking for in your other case," Rowland pleaded with the police chief. "Besides, when Brian gets here, I can just have him find what I need inside of your brain. And, believe me, it isn't a pleasant feeling when someone forces their way into your thoughts."

Rowland knew that Brian had the ability to read thoughts when people think them easily, but hates to have to pry thoughts that are hidden in the mind. It can be very dangerous for the mind in which the thoughts are concealed. So, Brian rarely does it; and Rowland would never really ask him to risk it with Jeff. Of course, people tend to think of the subject in question if he would ask them about the topic. It's kind of a tricky way to get information that someone doesn't want you to know. Unless of course they trained their minds to be better at shielding. Rowland knew firsthand how hard it was to keep thoughts from coming to the surface when Brian asked you questions with his mind. It had taken Rowland himself awhile to master his blocking; and that wasn't always a guarantee. This was getting to be more and more apparent as of late.

Jeff, not knowing the extent of Brian's power to read minds and how far Rowland was willing push the issue, decided he may as well tell Rowland what he had been hiding from him. Jeff was afraid that Brian's tactics may not be very pleasant. "Fine, I will tell you. About two weeks ago, three men from our area turned up missing. I kept it out of the papers while we have been investigating to protect their wives from being harassed by the media. The only link we could find between the three men, other than the fact that they were all married, was that they were known adulterers. However, that was in their pasts. The three of them had turned over a new leaf and attended church regularly up until their disappearance.

"None of the men knew one another according to the family and friends that we had contacted.

"All three men went missing simultaneously, but from three different locations. There were no witnesses to any of the disappearances. Well, no witnesses that have come forward. It was almost like these guys just vanished from the face of the earth or something. There wasn't even a trail for our dogs to follow."

"Two weeks ago, huh," Rowland said the thought out load. His brain was working hard to figure out where these disappearances would fit in with the recent murder and the problems that he had been having with the mental invader. "Two weeks ago was around the time the creature started invading my thoughts. At first it was happening only while I was sleeping. I would have vivid dreams of mauling people I knew and loved. I would wake up drenched in sweat with Stephen staring at me with worry in his eyes. Who or whatever is doing this to me has gotten stronger since the first attacks. I'm not sure how much longer I can continue to battle it for control of my mind."

"There is more that I haven't told you about the three missing men," Jeff continued. "We found them a few days after they went missing. They had washed up on the bank of the Mississippi River. All three had drowned and there were no signs of struggle on any of the men. It was as if they had just jumped in to the river and drowned themselves. We hadn't said anything because it appeared that all three men had committed suicide. Though, the likelihood that three fully functional men, with no history of mental illness, would take their own lives in the same instance. That, with the fact that it was done simultaneously without the victims even knowing one another, was causing this to rapidly be calked up as another cold case for stack. However, that is what our reports read as of now."

"I really think that this may be connected with the other disturbances we have been having in the area," Rowland told Jeff, wishing that he wasn't sure he was right. "I just wish that I could figure out what it is that could be doing this. Hopefully Brian has found something out."

Jeff applied the brake and slowed to a stop on the edge of town. "Well, this is where we found the body. Let's see if you can pick-up the trial of these creatures that murdered that poor woman."

As soon as Rowland stepped out of the vehicle, he smelled the now familiar scent of the creatures that had murdered that woman. He could also smell blood and meat that was still fairly fresh. Rowland knew that following these creatures would be nearly impossible. He could tell that these creatures must prefer flying.

"Bad news, Jeff," Rowland informed the officer that was standing beside him. "It appears that these creatures do prefer to stick to the air. And judging by how rapid the scent trail fades from the ground I'd say these beings are very fast. This investigation may not be as easy as we had thought, or hoped might be a better term. Then again, when do we ever catch a break with supernatural beings involved."

"It's alright Rowland. I'm sure that you and your pack will keep your noses out for any signs of these things, along with your eyes and ears of course," Jeff said, clearly disappointed. "We will get whatever is doing this. Then you, your pack, and our town will be safe again."

"I hope so."

Rowland, while Jeff had made his little pep talk, had already begun formulating a plan in which to track down at least one of the things that they were looking for. He was going to have to push Brian's abilities to their limits. He was going to find out if, since Brian had a similar gift, he could trace a connection back to its source; even though the source itself was out of his range. If so, he would be able to figure out who had committed at least one of the crimes. Okay, invading some one's mind isn't exactly a crime; but it should be.

Of course, this plan did have a fall back. He would have to let his guard down and allow this thing that has been attacking his mind to do so again. And, he wasn't even sure if Brian could do a trace on the mind that was doing this until Rowland himself had already given into this being.

Okay, so the plan was flawed. If Brian couldn't do a trace, then he hoped that he was strong enough to fight off the mental invader. If he couldn't fight it off, then it wouldn't matter at all what happens because this being will have won. Which means his entire pack would be doomed. Not to mention the damage that someone that wasn't right in the head could cause with a pack this size at their disposal. Werewolves in general would be a bad enough threat to the human population in the wrong hands; Rowland's pack had the added problem of being blessed with extra abilities. The damage would be catastrophic.

12: A BAD IDEA

'J eff,' Brian said with his mind searching out to find the mind of his alpha's companion. 'We just hit town. Where are you guys?'

'Rowland and I are at the place that the murder had taken place,' Jeff replied while projecting their location to Brian. 'There had been a few disappearances that had started around the time Rowland's mind starting being invaded. We found those bodies a few days later. Then this murder happened; and Rowland thinks that all these events are somehow related.'

'After what I found out from Marzipan, I think that you may be right. Though, I hope to God that you aren't.' Brian was just about to end the connection with Jeff's mind when he caught a glimpse of Rowland's calculated face. 'Rowland has the look that says he has come up with a plan, and not a good one.'

'We will talk about that later. Right now I need you guys to hurry up and get here and fill us in on what you found out,' Jeff told Brian before he could continue his complaint about the foolhardy plan that Rowland had more than likely formulated.

"Shit! Our Alpha is going to get everyone killed," Brian exclaimed after he severed the connection with Jeff's mind. "Rowland had the look of a dead man walking when I caught a glimpse of him from Jeff's perspective."

Ashlee whimpered in the backseat. He knew that Brian cared about Rowland and that he would follow him no matter what. Wondering what kind of plan Rowland could have formulated to make Brian so agitated was hurting his head. He knew that Brian wouldn't fill him in on the plan, even if he had known exactly what that plan was, till he absolutely needed to know. Brian may not be his favorite person; but he was very loyal to his friends and his pack. Ashlee respected him for that, though he wouldn't exactly consider him a friend.

"It's ok Ashlee," Brian told him. "I will find a way to convince Rowland to figure out a different plan if it's too dangerous. Though, for the life of me; I can't figure out what could have made such a cavalier look appear on his face. Though, I have a few guesses that may be close, and I don't like any of them."

Ashlee leaned forward and placed his head on Brian's shoulder to try to comfort the other man. He had a bad feeling in the pit of his stomach that things were going to go very bad over the next day or so. Yet, somehow he knew that they would get through this alright.

"I hope that you're right Ash," Brian said to the wolf resting his head on his shoulder. Brian reached up and scratched Ashlee behind the ears.

Ashlee arched an eyebrow at Brian. He hated that everything that he thought was an open book for Brian to read. 'So, how long have you been listening to my thought process?'

'Long enough,' Brian informed Ashlee.

Ashlee sat back in the seat and gave Brian a leer that would make a normal person shiver and cringe. Of course, it may have been the fact that it was coming from a Giant wolf that gave the stare that effect.

Noticing the look that Ashlee was giving Brian, Darvis realized that he must have missed something during their mental conversation. He didn't like having things kept from him; and that had only gotten worse since he had become a cop.

"What the hell did I miss," Darvis asked, glancing sideways at Brian.

Brian shifted slightly in his seat until his back was straight and the rest of him went ridged. "It's nothing that you need to worry about. It is pack business and doesn't have anything to do with the case. If Rowland deems that you should know, and then we shall tell you," Brian said in response to the question that Darvis had asked him.

Darvis could tell by Brian tone that he wasn't getting any information out of him until he was given the okay by Rowland. For once, since he had met the wolf in the backseat, he wished that Ashlee was in human form. Though, the ride home had been more peaceful; he knew that Ashlee would have divulged the answer he wanted, even if Brian told him not to do so. Come to think of it, he was sure Brian telling him not to tell would have made Ashlee reveal the info that much quicker.

Darvis glanced in the mirror to find Ashlee staring back at him. He wished that he had Brian's ability of telepathy to understand what the sad look that the wolf was giving him meant.

'You don't have to be so hard on him, Brian,' Ashlee projected at the man in the passenger seat of the truck. He liked Darvis and knew that he was just wanting to help if he could.

'I, unlike you, do what's best for the pack and don't let my emotions get in the way of that. Until you start putting aside you empathy for humans, you will never be more than a submissive wolf,' Brian thought with a mental growl. Though, he knew that wasn't entirely true. After all, Brian himself was a big softy through all of the tough guy exterior.

'Rowland isn't heartless, and I know that you aren't either. You are starting to sound like a monster with thoughts like that going through your mind.'

'Sorry, I do value other people's lives. Be it the lives of wolf or human. I'm just a little on edge lately. My life is finally going the way that I want; and I'm kinda happy. I'm just waiting for the other shoe to drop. It seems that anytime I start experiencing happiness, things go south shortly after. You wouldn't understand. The only reason that your life has any hard times is because you mess it up. Karma should be working full force again you, but it seems to target me. Rowland used to have the same out look on life till he met Stephen. Now he has gotten weaker and let his guard down enough that this mage has had a chance to penetrate his mental defenses. Thus, I have to be more of a hard ass to make up for it,' Brian told Ashlee, bowing his head to stop the tears that were trying to force their way out of his eyes. He would never admit that he was jealous of the fact that Rowland found someone to make him happy. He had taken for granite that Rowland was always going to be like him. Now, he can see how wrong he had been.

'Don't be hard on Rowland for finding a companion. Of all of us, he deserves it the most. He had always gone out of his way to help me; giving up his own happiness to ensure that I had mine. I regret that I had thrown that back in his face many times. The truth is, I was trying to push him away so that he may find happiness himself. Yet, he stayed faithful to me till he became a beast,' Ashlee began. 'And now, here you are complaining about him being happy. You could find the person that makes you feel that way. I mean, you have feelings for Kristie. And if your nose wasn't up your own ass, you could smell that she is into you also. This not finding happiness crap is all on you to change it,' Ashlee thought, a bit more sternly than he would have if he had been in human form.

"I should be pissed at you, but I'm not for a change. Maybe you're right. Do you have her number by chance," Brian asked out load. He avoided a look from Darvis that said plainly he was still not happy with information not being divulged unto him.

'Are you kidding? She's a chick, thus I got her digits.' Ashlee informed Brian with a grin spread across his wolf face. 'I will give it to you on one condition.'

'What would that be?'

'That you try not to break any of my bones for a while.'

Brian thought about it for a moment; weighing the options he had. On the one hand, he gets the girl that he likes for a change. On the other hand, he wouldn't be able to take his aggression out on Ashlee anymore. 'Sure, I will try not to pound on you for a while.'

'Ah, close enough. Her number is: 1-606-555-1484. Now you owe me,' Ashlee said, clearly proud of himself.

'I will only agree with you on that if it works. However, we have you talk with Rowland first.'

As Brian finished the thought, the car began to slow to a stop. He could see that Jeff had pulled his squad car off into the field. "Pull up behind Jeff's squad car," Brian instructed Darvis, though he had already begun doing just that before Brian had even spoke.

As Darvis put the truck into park, he could see Jeff standing next to a crouching man that he took to be Rowland. He unbuckled his seatbelt and opened the driver's side door. Before he had a chance to get out of the truck, a blur of motion went flying past him, out the open door.

As he stepped out, Darvis stared at the wolf that had rushed to beat him out of the vehicle. "Show off," Darvis said with a sneer at Ashlee. He knew that Ashlee felt compelled to show that he was dominant to a human; but that didn't change the fact that it was annoying.

"Come on you two," Brian called from over where Jeff and Rowland stood.

"Why does it feel like I'm the only one that can't move as fast as a blur? Rudi is really going to have a field day when he gets control of his change," Darvis said as he approached the others.

"Don't worry," Rowland said as Darvis stopped in front of him. "Jeff is still slower than you; that's gotta count for something."

"Real funny, dog breath," Jeff replied. "Can we get this little shindig underway?"

"Right," Rowland agreed. "Brian, fill us in on what you found out."

Brian filled Jeff and Rowland in on the information about what type of evil sons-a-bitches they could be facing in the days to come. And he didn't sugar coat it either.

"Ok, now it's your turn Rowland. I could see the wheels a turning when I was linked to Jeff's mind. What is your plan," Brian asked.

Rowland told them of his plan to let the mage in and have Brian track the connection back to its host.

"Rowland, this mage is powerful enough to affect a banshee. Do you really think that you should let him seize control of your mind at will in the off chance that I might be able to track him," Brian questioned his Alpha for the first time.

"Listen, I know that this plan sucks. In fact, I'm not sure I can fight free of this mage's control again. He is getting more and more powerful by the day. In another day or so it won't matter whether we can trace his mental signal back to him. If we wait, he gets what he wants any way. And we lose everything."

"I'm sorry, I hadn't realized that this guys strength was increasing at such a rate," Brian said to Rowland. "Lets do whatever it takes to bring these things to justice."

"Alright," Rowland told his second. He had always been impressed with Brian's undying faith in him. Rowland hoped that things would work out in the end, but it was a long shot.

"What should we do," Jeff asked Rowland as if he had heard the thoughts of doubt that had just gone through his mind.

"Pray that my plan works," Rowland told him. "If we fail; go to Marzipan. I'm sure she will be able to stop this guy before he can do too much damage."

"Sure thing," Jeff responded to Rowland.

Turning to Darvis, Jeff signaled that they should leave.

Like the good officer he was, Darvis turned and headed for the squad car without another word.

13: CALM BEFORE THE STORM

fter Jeff and Darvis pulled away, Rowland turned to Ashlee and told him to head back to his house to change and let Kristie know what they planned to do.

However, before Ashlee had a chance to take off, Brian stopped him. "Rowland. Can I be the one to go back to fill Kristie and the others in on the plan? I can get there faster and no one could challenge what I say to them," Brian requested.

"Um, sure. I guess it doesn't really matter. And you may be right, you have more authority than Ashlee. Not to mention the fact that you can convince any doubters by projecting my plan into their thoughts," Rowland said, agreeing with Brian.

Ashlee looked at Brian with questioning eyes. 'Why do you want to do this? It's grunt work.'

'Because, that will give me an opportunity to talk to Kristie. In other words, I don't owe you for the number,' Brian said via mind to Ashlee.

Turning to Rowland, Brian said, "I will meet you at your house."

Brian turned to leave; and smacked Ashlee upside the head as he passed the wolf.

'Ouch! What was that for?'

'For trying to blackmail me into having to be nice to you,' Brian explained as he disappeared into the woods that surrounded the field.

Once Brian was gone, Rowland headed toward Brian's truck to head back home. "Come on Ashlee," Rowland called to the wolf. "I will order some pizza; that way it will be there when we get to the house."

At hearing the mention of food, Ashlee's ears perked up and he bolted for the truck.

Ashlee sat in the passenger seat, wagging his tail, as Rowland hopped into the driver's seat. Rowland reached over and patted his friend on top of the head as he hit the gas. "You did good tonight. I really do get the feeling that you have more potential as a wolf than anyone gives you credit for. I'm ashamed to admit that I was one of the ones that was a little doubtful at first," Rowland said with sadness heavy in his voice.

Ashlee whimpered to the remark from Rowland and licked his hand. Rowland glanced at Ashlee and sighed. "You and I have never been good at being angry with one another. Maybe that's why we have always been such good friends," Rowland told Ashlee. "At least in this form you can't talk back."

Ashlee snapped at Rowland's hand in a playful manner.

Laughing, Rowland rubbed Ashlee's head a little rougher and said, "Calm down there Cujo, I was only joking. Well, sort of."

Ashlee looked at his alpha and rolled his eyes. He missed the way Rowland was before he became a werewolf. No body else seemed to notice that he had change. It was a subtle difference from the way he was to the way he is. Mostly it was the way he held himself. Body language played a large part in werewolf society; however, it was even before he had wolfed-out himself that Ashlee had begun noticing the difference. He had thought becoming a wolf himself would bring their friendship back to the way things used to be, but he had been wrong.

He thought back to the trouble that he and Rowland used to get into when they were younger while growing-up in a small town similar to Albany in southern Illinois. Ashlee had moved to Albany as Rowland's roommate at first. And how things started to fall apart once Rowland became a monster. While lost in thought, Ashlee didn't even seem to notice the time that had transpired until they were pulling into Rowland's driveway.

Ashlee looked over at Rowland eagerly, waiting for him to open the door. The lack of hands made it impossible even for a werewolf to open a car door handle.

Finally, after a few minutes to collect his thoughts, Rowland decided it was time to go inside. He hopped out of the truck and let Ashlee, who ran into the yard to relieve himself, out of the vehicle. After finishing, Ashlee kicked dirt on the spot where he had just relieved himself and then padded his way up to the door of the house. For the first time since becoming a werewolf, he couldn't wait to be in human form again.

As soon as the door opened, which it did just before Rowland and Ashlee reached it (you just can't sneak up on a telepath), Ashlee flew upstairs to change and get dressed. Rowland was always prepared for a day like today with two sets of clothing in every member of his pack.

"Hello boss man," Rudi greeted Rowland after having to quickly dodge the giant wolf that had rushed threw the door before it was opened more than a crack wide enough for the beast to fit through.

"Hey, Rudi," Rowland replied. "How are you adjusting to this new way of life thus far?"

"Pretty good so far," Rudi responded with a smile; though the smile quickly faded as he continued. "Well, I did lose my temper once so far. And it was over something small. Normally it would have annoyed me, maybe make me mad. Yet, for some reason, I completely lost it."

"That's just part of the change. Werewolves aren't just rumored to have short tempers; we actually do tend to be more on the cranky side," Rowland told the young police officer. "You will learn to control it. But, until you do, you probably shouldn't go around to many humans. Wouldn't want to go into a rage when there isn't anyone around to stop you. And the presence of other werewolves is a natural way of calming the beast within; as long as the other wolf isn't challenging your wolf."

"Oh, should I tell my fiancé? I mean, she's going to be worried," Rudi asked.

"Well, normally we limit it to wives as far as revealing the secret to; but I think we can make an exception. After all, she soon will become your wife and you wouldn't want to keep secrets from her," Rowland told Rudi. "On one condition…"

"Anything! She means the world to me."

"Well, the stipulation is that the entire pack gets to come to the wedding. Oh, and you and your fiancé have to have dinner with Stephen and myself next weekend," Rowland told Rudi, who's face lit up at hearing the stipulations that Rowland set.

"We would love to have the pack at our wedding. Of course, I will have to check the Lunar Calendar to be sure that I don't have to reschedule the big day," Rudi replied laughing.

Rowland laughed along with the new wolf at the little joke he had made; though, Rowland knew that it was really no laughing matter. If the wedding was scheduled for a night of a full moon, it would need to be pushed back. No way would he risk the exposure of their kind over something as trivial and out dated as marriage.

'Your just bitter because you and Stephen can't get married in our fine state.' Brian had appeared in the door way leading from the kitchen without Rowland even hearing his approach. Brian shook his head, 'You would have heard me if you weren't lost in your own thoughts. Of course, I wouldn't know this if someone had their shields up. You are being careless, my old friend.'

'Sorry Brian,' Rowland replied. 'I have a lot on my mind, as you well know. Besides; check my shielding again and you will find it is intact. Only one telepath aloud.'

And without another word, Rowland reconstructed his mental defenses, blocking Brian out completely. As he did, he noticed a strange noise coming from his kitchen. It sounded a little like the giggling of a giddy little school girl.

Intrigued, he headed for the doorway in which Brian still stood. "What's going on in there," Rowland asked Brian.

"Well, apparently I made Kristie's night," Brian said with a wink. "When I got here, I asked her on a date. And, before she could answer, I kissed her. It's so not like me to be so forward with a girl; but I could smell the desire that I felt for her being mimicked by her own desire for me. Needless to say, she said yes."

"Wow! That's great! I was wondering when the two of you were going to realize that you wanted each other," Rowland said, placing a hand on Brian's shoulder and laughing. "We should celebrate tonight."

"What about your plan? Shouldn't that be our concern," Brian asked his alpha.

"Don't be stupid. This is far more important than going through with my plan. I mean, if my plan fails, when would we celebrate," Rowland told Brian with a lighthearted tone that really didn't fit the tension that he felt. He knew that his scent would give away the fact that he was lying. A werewolf's nose was better than any lie detector test. Only one person had ever been able to fool Rowland's nose, and that had been Marzipan. However, she had centuries to practice.

"Rowland, I know that you are good at keeping your emotions in check sometime in order to make everyone else's life better; but this is one time that you do not need to do this," Brian told Rowland as a friend more than a pack mate.

"Please, Brian, I have to do this. If we let this guy, this mage, keep us from having this be a happy moment; then he has already won. And I will not allow that," Rowland said, surprised by how true his words rang. "We need this more than you may realize right now. If my plan fails, let it be tomorrow. That way you and Kristie will have at least one night to be happy together."

"If you think it is best; then I will back you 100%," Brian informed Rowland. "Who knows? Maybe the morale boost will help us to achieve our goal."

After reluctant agreement on Brian's part, he finally was seeing eye to eye with Rowland. He wanted more than anything to get the bastards that were causing strife in his life. Which would in turn, give him a chance to see where things took him with Kristie.

As Brian and Rowland entered the kitchen, the laughter ceased instantly. Kimberly, Olivia, Leslie, and Sherry were all huddled together by the kitchen counter with Kristie at the center. Rowland knew right away that they had interrupted a girl talk moment. He wondered where the other male pack members had gotten off to.

"Brian, where are the guys at?"

"They went for a run at my request," Brian explained. "I tried getting the girls to go with them; but they hadn't gotten far when Kristie called them back after I asked her on a date." Brian began blushing as he finished explaining.

All the girls let out a long "Awwww" to express the "cuteness" of how Brian was reacting. Of course, it could have something to do with the fact that Kristie had began to blush as well.

"Had you filled them in on my plan before you sent them away," Rowland asked.

"Um, no," Brian said, bowing his head. He didn't want to see the look of disappointment in his alpha's face after he had failed to follow a simple order like relaying a message. "I'm sorry."

"No big deal," Rowland told Brian, which took Brian by surprise. "Now we can have a fun evening without having my stupid idea ruin it."

"Thanks," Brian said to Rowland. "It means a lot that you are putting everything on hold for me to have at least one night of fun before we risk our lives."

"Ah, HELLO," Kristie belted from across the room. Her giddiness had apparently run out. "We aren't deaf you know. We can hear everything that you two are talking about. What's this plan that you have and how dangerous is it?"

"Don't worry about it tonight Kristie. We will have way to much to worry ourselves with tomorrow," Rowland instructed her, using his Alpha Call on her for the first time.

Kristie looked as if she had been smack in the face when the order hit her. She didn't protest however, not that she could even if she had wanted to. Kristie may not have ever been in the military, but she was very good at following orders. Especially the order that she couldn't contest to.

A moment later, the door bell rang. It hadn't surprised any of the wolves in the house, since they could smell the pizza a block away.

Rowland answered the door and paid for the pizzas. It took the delivery man two trips to bring the mound of pies to the door. This was one of the down falls of being a were-anything. Having such a high metabolism meant that you had to consume what felt like truck loads of food a day. It wasn't so bad when in wolf form because they could always hunt down deer or other wild animals.

When Rowland returned to the kitchen he could tell that none of the wolves had eaten since their run earlier that day. As soon as the pizzas were set down, Rudi reached for a slice. This was a bad idea in a normal pack because they ate in order of dominance. However, Rowland was too tired to uphold pack protocol. So, the new guy got to keep his hand for now. Brian and Kristie shot Rowland a look of surprise because he normally would have corrected the breach in protocol; though, not violently. At least not the first time.

They all ate in silence. It took the wolves less than fifteen minutes to go through all twenty-five pizzas.

After taking a moment to allow their stomachs to settle, Rowland finally broke the silence. "The rest of you can take off. There will be a pack meeting at ten am tomorrow to discuss this plan of mine," Rowland informed the rest with a little more of a dismissive attitude than he had intended.

Rowland went to the kitchen table as the others began to leave. He was followed shortly by Brian, who sat next to Kristie.

After everyone was gone, with the exception of Ashlee who was passed out upstairs. And, even though he hadn't seen him, Rowland knew that Stephen was there. He could smell him, yes; but even without having a great sniffer he could feel his presence. The bond between himself and Stephen had surpassed anything that he had ever known. If Stephen stubs his toe, Rowland shares his pain. Not really feeling his pain like the expression, but literally sharing the pain by lessening what Stephen felt. It was only recently that he and Stephen had noticed this change. Rowland wondered if it would increase if he turned Stephen.

Almost as if he could sense Rowland thinking of him, Stephen made his way into the kitchen and over to the chair beside Rowland.

Stephen reached over and grabbed Rowland's hand. "Welcome home," Stephen whispered as though the other two people in the room couldn't hear him if he did. "I have been worried about you all day."

Rowland leaned in and kissed him on the cheek. "You don't need to worry about me."

"I know, but it's in my nature."

Stephen looked up and seemed to notice for the first time that his sister and Brian were sitting opposite himself and Rowland. "Um, hey sis. Brian."

Smirking at Stephen, Brian nodded his hello.

"So, have you heard yet," Kristie asked her brother.

Stephen tilted his head slightly to the side in a gesture common to a dog more than a human. After a moment, he smiled and exclaimed, "Oh My God! You two finally go wise and are going to go on a date with one another. This is such great news."

Stephen jumped from his seat to run around to the other side of the table to hug both Brian and Kristie.

Rowland couldn't help but laugh at the look on Brian's face when Stephen had embraced him. Brian was less homophobic than most of Rowland's friends. He just didn't care to be hugged by anyone.

"Let's open a bottle of wine and sit around in the living room and talk," Stephen said. "This will give the two of you a chance to get to know one another."

"Stephen," Kristie interrupted her brother before he could build up enough steam in his rant. "We already know each other."

"Yeah. As a pack you do," Rowland interjected. "But I'd wager that you two know nothing personal about the other person. Especially since Brian is clueless when it comes to your mind, Kristie."

Rowland and Stephen shared a laugh at the expense other two in the room. They had over come the 'getting to know' part of the relationship quickly themselves. Though, Rowland had a feeling that Brian would find it more difficult than he had in his relationship because he was used to getting inside peoples minds.

"You guys are right," Brian agreed. "Kristie and I never really talked, even as pack members. I was too nervous to strike up conversation with her before. If Ash hadn't said anything I may still be beating around the bush."

"Damn," Stephen swore. "I was thinking that you had gotten wise yourself. You have proven me wrong."

"Very funny little brother," Kristie added. She enjoyed pointing out to her twin that she was born minutes before he was.

"Okay. I think that's enough of the taunting them on finally realizing that they like one another," Rowland stated, growing tired of the same conversation being repeated in different words. "Let's go ahead and call it a night. Brian, you and Kristie can have the spare bedroom to talk and crash. Stephen, let's go hit the hay, I'm tired. Though, it will be kind of cramped with Ashlee in our bed."

On that note, the four of them got up from the table and left the kitchen. Rowland thought to himself how much he loved being alpha sometimes. Having authority over people had perks.

Rowland and Stephen bid goodnight to Brian and Kristie; and headed upstairs to bed.

14: Flaw in the Plan

shlee woke before anyone else in the house. He made his way down to the kitchen hoping to find some leftovers in the fridge, since he slept through dinner the night before. He was not lucky, which didn't surprise him. He was kind of used to this by now. Being the low man in the ranks meant he had to learn to fend for himself. This meant he had had to learn to cook, which he was not happy about.

Since the leftover pizza idea was a flop, Ashlee began raiding the cabinets. He lucked out when he found a box of Bisquick to make pancakes.

He measured enough for ten pancakes and then decided that wouldn't be enough if the others woke up before he finished helping himself. So, he went a head and started cooking the whole box; eating them as he went to get his stomach to stop growling.

After he had a nice stack of pancakes prepared; Ashlee went to take a shower to get the wet fur smell off of himself.

While Ashlee was getting clean, Rowland and Stephen made their way down stairs to a breakfast that was prepared so recently, that even Stephen's human sense of smell could detect.

"Wow," Rowland exclaimed when he entered his kitchen to find the pancakes stacked ten high on several different plates. "Ash really out did himself this time. Normally he comes over and stays because I make breakfast for us. This is amazing."

"Yeah," Stephen said with a bit of exaggeration in his tone. Stephen tended to be cranky in the morning if he didn't get his caffeine fix. "All I know is that I'm grateful that he made coffee, but I'm so not cleaning his dishes."

Rowland stepped up behind his boyfriend and wrapped his arms around him. He leaned down and lightly kissed his neck just below his ear. "Did I ever tell you that you are very cute when you're cranky?"

"Yes," Stephen said, though his tone said that he clearly wanted to say, 'FUCK YOU.'

"I love you," Rowland said. He squeezed Stephen a little bit tighter before letting him go.

"I think I'm going to be sick," Ashlee said. Rowland had heard him coming into the room just after he embraced Stephen. Stephen, however, had been startled when Ash spoke.

Of course, being the ball of witty retorts that Stephen was in the mornings, he simply said, "Well, guess I will stick to coffee for my breakfast if your cooking is bad enough to make a werewolf ill."

Ashlee just glared at Stephen for a long minute. Finally, after what felt like an eternity to Rowland, who just stood there watching his best friend stare down his boy friend. He knew that, in the unlikely event that Ash would try to attack, he would have the upper hand. Perks of being an Alpha.

"You're right. He is cranky when he hasn't had his coffee," Ashlee stated. "And, fyi, the pancakes are great. I just can't stomach public displays of affection."

"You don't like public displays of affection," Rowland asked in a facetious tone. "You have made out with how many girls in front of me. Often times you would do it to try to make me jealous, though it never worked. Once, you had a girl give you a blow job while I was sitting right next to you. Like you have room to talk about p.d.a."

"I think that crankiness stuff is contagious," Ashlee said.

"No," Stephen chimed in. "I think that you are mad that we are in love and happy. From what I have heard about your past relationships, no wonder you are jealous. Constant fighting and bitching at one another doesn't make for a very healthy relationship. Also, maybe you should have them psychoanalyzed before you jump into the sack. Just a thought."

"What would you know!"

"Ashlee, calm down," Rowland warned. "You do not want to lose your temper right now."

"You have room to talk," Ashlee began, gathering steam. "All you do lately is complain about one thing or another. Never about your relationship; but there's always something. So don't stand there acting like you are so perfect. You are no better than me."

"I never said I was better than anyone," Rowland said in a somber tone. "And everyone has their problems. All Stephen was trying to say is, if it bothers you to see us together, turn your head. However, I know that it doesn't bother you. And that you really are happy for us. You just have a unique way of showing it."

"But he said that my past relationships didn't work," Ashlee said as though Stephen wasn't there.

"Well, they obviously didn't work if they are past relationships," Rowland pointed out, which made Stephen snicker. "Also, if its what you want in a relationship, what's it matter what other people think. It's not like Stephen and I don't fight. We just talk it out and find a middle ground that we can agree on."

"Oh," Ashlee said. "Well, shit! Now I feel like a complete dumb ass."

"Ash, you aren't a complete dumb ass, only about ninety percent dumb ass," Stephen told him.

"Oh, now you're a fucking comedian," Ash said, trying to sound angry again; but he failed miserably because his stern face broke as laughter began.

The three guys sat at the kitchen table in silence for a while. None of them daring to talk out of fear of setting the others off.

About an hour went by without a word being said; until Brian and Kristie woke up. Almost immediately Rowland and Ashlee could hear the almost silent laughter of Brian and Kristie as they said their good mornings. Rowland was pleased to hear the way they greeted one another already. Ashlee, however, was a little annoyed and couldn't keep it off his face.

A few minutes later, Brian and Kristie appeared in the kitchen, moving with their otherworldly speed. They both rushed to the table without even a wave of good morning, and began eating. Part way through the stuffing of their faces, they realized that everyone's eyes were on them.

"Hey, guys," Kristie greeted them. "Who made the pancakes? They are amazing."

"That would be me," Ashlee admitted, raising his hand, with a hint of pride at the fact that everyone ended up liking his cooking.

"Wow! Ash-hole can cook," Brian said tauntingly, with a wink at Rowland and Stephen. "Who knew you could do anything right."

"Thanks, I think. I'm sure that there was a compliment in there some where if I think about it," Ashlee said, trying to be the bigger man. Well, more well behaved werewolf to be exact.

"Don't think to much, you will hurt yourself. But yes, it was a compliment. Thanks for breakfast."

Taken aback by the fact that Brian had not only complimented him, but thanked him as well; left Ashlee speechless. And that was something that rarely happened. Ashlee was the kind of person that spoke their mind without any regard for what others would think. At one point in time, it was because he had had a little too much to drink. Now, since werewolves metabolize alcohol faster than it can be consumed, no one knew why he still was having problems censoring his thought to mouth process.

Ashlee stood up and headed for the kitchen door. Just as he reached the doorway he turned to Rowland and asked, "Should I let them in?" As he finished the question, there came a knock on the door. Everyone, with the exception of Stephen, knew that the other pack members were approaching about two minutes before the knocking started.

"I hate being the only one in the room without superhuman abilities," Stephen complained with a pout on his face. "Why wont you change me already?"

"If what I have planned in order to catch these bad guys works, I promise to change you after the danger is over," Rowland swore to his significant other. "Besides, I think it's kind of cute when you get all whinny because you are still only human."

"That's a bullshit reason not to have changed me already," Stephen spat at Rowland, his temper flaring up again. "This must be one dangerous fucking plan you have come up with to have you promising things that you really don't want to do."

"Dangerous. You could call it that," Rowland said to Stephen. Rowland would never tell Stephen, but he liked it when he was angry. He felt like he could relate to Stephen better. Though, if he turned Stephen, how much worse would his anger get?

"IF YOU GET YOURSELF KILLED, I WILL FIND SOMEONE TO ANIMATE YOUR ASS SO I CAN KICK IT," Stephen shouted at him, getting to his feet and storming out of the house.

"What was that about," Kristie asked Rowland. She loved her twin brother and had been happy that her alpha loved him as well. Yet, she had never seen Stephen get so pissed off before.

"Well, he and I have been having a little bit of a disagreement when it concerns me changing him," Rowland explained.

"Oh, I see. Why is it making him so upset though?"

"I think that he feels powerless to help me since I have been under constant attack the last few weeks."

"That's just dumb. All of us have been helpless to do anything," Kristie said, her own temper getting the best of her.

"Well, I'm hoping that one of you will be able to help," Rowland said with a glance at Brian. "Let's go into the living room and I will explain the plan in more detail."

The three of them stood up and headed into the other room. The entire pack was already sitting around all over the living room when they finally made their way in to join them.

Rowland stood in the middle of them and went over his plan to try to trace the link between himself and the mage. Everyone sat motionless as he explained the danger involved.

When he finally finished, Kristie stood up and screamed at him, "How can you do this? Don't you care about my brother at all? He only wants to be changed to be closer to you."

"Really, Kristie, I do love your brother. I made him pissed off at me because I couldn't stand having him here when I went over this plan." Rowland was on the verge of tears when he was trying to explain why he had intentionally angered Stephen. He loved the guy more than he had loved anyone in his entire life.

"Seriously. Can you two leave it be for a while? We've got a job to do; and the longer we wait, the stronger this magician will become," Brian began, trying to nip the little spat in the butt before it got out of hand. "Besides, if anyone can complain it's Rowland or myself. We are the ones at risk."

"Your right. I'm sorry. I just worry about my brother," Kristie said, calming quickly.

"Well, if you two are done, can we begin."

"Sure thing," Rowland stated, agreeing with Brian that time was of the essence.

Rowland sat in his most comfortable recliner and began to lower his mental shields.

Brian, who was monitoring the whole time as Rowland relaxed himself, noticed right away that the strange presence had already began to weave it's way into Rowland's thoughts. It was so smooth of a presence that Rowland himself didn't notice until it latched onto his thoughts and began the process of seizing control.

Brian, baffled by how easily the intruder had entered Rowland's mind, almost forgot why he was monitoring in the first place. When he finally remember, he realized that he could detect a thread connecting whatever it was to Rowland's mind. It wasn't a thread that one could see. Rather, it was a metaphysical link that only a telepath could detect.

Upon *seeing* this thread, Brian began to follow it.

He didn't go alone. Dylan, Justin, and Zach followed shortly behind.

Once outside, Brian realized that this presence was based from the woods just behind Rowland's house. He was a little disturbed at the thought of someone this powerful being in their own back yard.

15: Out of Sight; Out of Their Minds

he signal began getting stronger as Brian and the others made their way toward their foe.

After a few seconds, Brian stopped so suddenly that Dylan ran into him.

"Hey, why are we stopping," Dylan asked as he stood up and brushed himself off after falling when he ran into Brian. Running into a werewolf was like running into a brick wall. And the stronger the werewolf, the tougher that wall appeared to be. "Are we that close?"

"Be quite a second and listen," Brian ordered.

Upon the command of the higher ranked wolf, the others stopped talking and perked their ears. It didn't take long for them to hear the rustle of leaves of foot steps behind them. Brian knew they weren't human because the foot falls were coming to rapidly. He put his nose to the air and was disappointed to notice that he and the others were not down wind from their pursuers.

"What the hell could be following us at this speed," Justin inquired.

"Well, I don't know what it is yet, but they will be within mind range in a second," Brian told him.

After a second, Brian closed his eyes and braced himself for the minds he was about to touch. He knew that there were many things that had mental defenses and didn't want to be incapacitated by one of them now.

A second went by and Brian could here familiar minds. 'Why couldn't they have just waited a second for us to go with them,' Ashlee thought.

By touching his mind, Brian knew that things had not gone well after he and the guys with him had left Rowland. Rowland had snapped and began to try and attack the other wolves in the living room where they had left him. He could see that there was an ambulance on its way to pick Rudi up because the kid had done the cop thing and tried to save everyone else. And, that Kristie and Kim had finally taken Rowland down for now by using their own special abilities.

'We should be glad that this mage hasn't gained enough control over Rowland to learn how to access his special talents. Or make him change. He could even command the entire pack if he wanted,' Brian said to Ashlee.

'How did you know that we were following you?'

'Well, stealth had never been your strong suit. And neither has brains.'

'Well, I never claimed to be smart,' Ashlee said with a mental smirk at Brian.

'If your going with us, get the lead out. I noticed that Nick, Wyatt, and Phillip are with you. I guess that after Rowland was over taken, it was decided that we would need more help,' Brian said. 'I will see you in a second.'

A moment later, the four other male wolves appeared in the small clearing in the woods. "Ok. Now we have to run at top speed because the signal is fading. It appears that the mage is leaving Rowland's mind for some reason. Which means, we are going in blind. And more than likely, they know that we are coming."

The wolves turned and ran in the direction of the rapidly fading thread of telepathic energy. Though it wasn't long before that trail went cold.

The hunting party slowed their pace to a trot, not knowing what may lie ahead. The adrenaline of the moment filled the air around them until it seemed like a haze that summer heat can cause at times.

Not long after they slowed their approach, Nick scented something that he had never smelled before. Nick had the best sense of smell in the entire pack while in human form. In wolf form, he was second only to the alpha himself. 'What kinda creature could this be,' Nick asked Brian via mind to mind communication.

'Shit,' Brian swore. 'I was hoping that we could avoid these creatures. All though, we do out number them.'

"Get ready boys. We are about to have company," Brian told the others. "Ashlee, Wyatt, Nick, and Phillip; get into wolf form. I'm not sure how their abilities work; but I'm hoping that we can take them out before they start to sing."

"Are you saying that the sirens are coming for us," Justin asked.

It was Dylan who answered, "No, he's telling us that Santa Claus is coming to bring us presents because we have been such good little boys. Of course he means the sirens are coming for us."

"Would you two cut it out and focus," Brian barked at them to get them to be quiet. "We aren't sure what these bitches are capable of."

There was a rustle of leaves and branches in front of the pack as five beautiful women entered the clearing before Ashlee, Wyatt, Nick, and Phillip had a chance to even begin their shift.

"Hello gentlemen," said the woman in the front of the group. "My name is Tangia. And these are my sisters. Their names are Clara, Mariana, Shiva, and Beta." Tangia pointed at the other women in turn as she introduced them.

Tangia was taller than her sisters, standing nearly six feet tall. She had blood red hair that hung to the middle of her back in long flowing waves that reflected the light from the sun in a shimmering way that no human's hair ever could. She was athletic in build and clearly the leader of her little family. Even with the hair shinning in a non-human way, she would have passed for human when wearing sunglasses. Her eyes were anything but human. They were the eyes of a predatory bird, similar to that of a hawk.

Clara and Mariana were clearly twins. Both having straight blonde hair that no dye job could ever match. Like their big sister, they had the same chestnut colored hawk eyes. Though, their bodies were build with more bust. They were made to attract and they accomplished their goal by looking like supermodels; or porn stars considering the leather tops and mini skirts.

Shiva and Beta were more exotic than the other three of their sisters. Shiva looked like she had African decent; though there was something more primitive mixed with it. Shiva appeared to be older than her other sisters. But, like with so many other supernatural creatures, one really couldn't tell their age by looking at them. Her hair was jet black which had a blue tint to it when the light played upon it. Her eyes were nearly black. They would have appeared truly black if the hair wasn't there to compare to. Her frame was smaller in every way compared to her sisters. Though, something in her eyes gave away how much more deadly she was than the others.

Lastly, there was Beta. She was very Asian in decent. Ancient Chinese by the way she held herself. The women in Ancient China had a strength that has not been matched by any male or female since. And Beta had that strength in spades. She kept her hair up in a tight bun that was held in place by what appeared to be jade pins. She was only inches taller than Shiva; and only slightly bigger in build. Though, it was obvious that it was all muscle.

"Hello ladies," Brian greeted them, suppressing a growl that was itching to come through his lips. "I am Brian of the Albany werewolf pack."

"You are not the Alpha," Clara stated.

"Well, no. Our Alpha was a bit preoccupied to make it."

"Our master will not be pleased to hear that," Mariana told him.

"Well, we wouldn't want to upset Mr. Psycho," Dylan told them, not bothering to hide his distaste. "And, while we're on the topic of psychos, why don't you ladies show us your real form. Honestly, you aren't fooling anyone here. I mean, we aren't exactly human."

"Trust me, you don't want to see our true form," Shiva spat with such a heavy accent that it was barely understood.

"Why not," Justin asked. "Are you afraid that one of us will have a feather allergy? Or, is it that you taste like chicken and you're worried we can't resist?"

The wolves all enjoyed a laugh at the expense of the creatures in front of them.

'Hurry up and shift already,' Brian projected at the four that he wanted in wolf form. 'They could decide to start their song at any moment and I'm not sure if our superhuman shit will help us at all against them.'

The four wolves that had been ordered to shift began to strip down in order to make the change a bit more comfortable. However, before they could finish taking their shirts off, Tangia began to hum a low tune that stopped them in their tracks. Soon, Tangia was joined by her sisters in song.

"Don't listen to them," Brian said to the others, though he knew it was already too late. He could feel the web of the sirens' spell as they sang to them. He only had a second to act before he too would become prey the lovely song. Though, it didn't leave him much time to think things through.

He threw himself at Tangia, doing a partial shift in the process. While lunging through the air, he used his telekinetic energy to thrust the other four sirens away, breaking their song. And, when he reached Tangia, he clamped his wolf fangs into her throat. He ripped at Tangia's trachea until his teeth clamped together.

Before Brian could recover from his death strike on Tangia, he felt talons ripping at his back.

He pushed his attacker away with a psychic pulse; and turned to face his foe. What he found was that the other four sirens had shifted to their true form.

Brian laughed at the sight and started to stalk in a circle. "Here birdie. I want to play," Brian said with a sinister grin spreading across his half human half wolf face. His eyes were glowing yellow, showing the excitement that his beast had from the taste of fresh blood.

He kept pacing, keeping all of the sirens within sight. He knew that these creatures were more than likely faster than he was. Though, he was sure that it wouldn't be by much; but he wasn't going to chance it.

"So, the dog has a bit of bite in him after all," Shiva said, throwing her head back in a laugh that sounded like a mix between that of a human and a bird. It was a strangely beautiful sound, though it seemed to promise pain or even death. "You will pay for killing our sister."

"Now Shiva. Why should we harm the poor man for defending himself," Clara told her sister, placing a calming hand on her shoulder. The look in her eyes said clearly that she was thinking terrible things. "We should let this dispute be settled by his brothers."

Brian hadn't notice the eerie feeling like he had people staring at him from behind. He began to turn slowly. He knew that he would excite the beasts of his brothers if he moved too quickly.

He reached out with his mind toward his pack mates; but he found that no one was home. It was almost as if they were lifeless beings; simple puppets being manipulated by the strings in their masters hands. And that's when he knew that he would either have to give up or fight the people that he cared for most.

"You win," Brian told the sirens. "I will not fight them. But this will not help your master get Rowland. He will come and fight you all until you cease to take breath again."

"Who said anything about wanting your Alpha? Our master's goal has always been to get *you* to come to him. He knew that you would find a way to track him. He also warned us against using our song on you. That you may take it as a hostel way of taking away your free will," Beta informed him.

"The others will come for us," Brian warned the sirens. "And when they do, you will be sorry."

"Ah, but for one little problem that you over looked," stated Mariana. "By the time they find you and these other little dogs; you will be their enemy as well."

Brian's eyes got big with shock as he realized the truth in what he had just heard.

'God help us.'

16. Search and Rescue

The covers on Rowland's couch where he had been lying after being knocked out began to move.

"I think he's waking up," Kim said with anxiety in her tone.

"Everyone be on guard. We don't know if he will be himself or try to attack us again," Kristie ordered.

Rowland could hear people moving around him and couldn't remember falling a sleep. He had no idea what had transpired after he gave in to the mage. All he knew for certain was that his head felt like it was splitting open.

"What's going on," Rowland asked as he forced his eye open. "Did I pass out after the mage took control?"

"You don't remember anything," Olivia asked. Her voice said that she wasn't sure that trusting the man on the sofa was such a good idea. After all, he had just tried to kill one pack member and hurt the rest before he was taken out.

"I remember dropping my mental defenses; then I woke up here," Rowland told them. He could sense their tension leave drop drastically. 'What had I done to make them so tense around me?'

Almost as though she had read his mind, Kristie began to explain how he had attacked Rudi without warning. How Ashlee had tackled him off Rudi. And, how Kim and herself had to use their abilities to subdue him.

"Oh, I see," Rowland said while looking at the floor. He didn't want to look at the others and see the distress that he had caused them still fresh in their eyes. However, he knew that he had to look. He was Alpha and it was his responsibility to keep the pack working. If he cowered after this, thus showing weakness, the power structure would crumble;

115

leaving the pack weak and vulnerable. Slowly, Rowland raised his head and looked the members of his pack that were left in the room in the eyes in turn; and said an apology to each of them.

"Rowland, we know that it wasn't you that did the attacking," Kim told him with tears in her eyes. "We were all worried about you. We thought that you were lost to us."

Rowland took a second the process that they knew it wasn't he who had done the attacking. After a moment of thinking, he realized that there had been no mention of the mission he had sent the others on. He also noticed that Ashlee and a few others were missing as well.

"Have any of you heard news from Brian and the others," Rowland asked.

Kristie turned a worried face to Rowland for the first time. She had always been the best in the pack at schooling her emotions. Even Brian, the ex-marine, couldn't hold a candle to how well Kristie could hide things. The fact that worry lines showed on her face was a sign that they hadn't heard any news and that she was afraid that something bad had happened.

Rowland didn't need an answer to his question after seeing Kristie's face. Instead, he got up and went to the phone. First, he called the hospital to check up on Rudi. Then, he called Jeff on his cell phone to tell him how terribly wrong the plan had gone.

After making his calls, he turned to face the woman of his pack, the only ones that he knew were safe.

"I think that my plan worked a bit too well. I fear that the mage may have anticipated the others finding him if he read my thoughts about the plan. That could be why he had used me as a weapon to try to hurt you," Rowland said, though it didn't entirely make sense to him. He was sure that the mage could have used him to take the other pack members over as well.

That's when it hit him. 'Maybe it hadn't been me all along. Maybe he just used me to lure the better part of the pack away from us and into a trap.'

"Shit," Rowland swore.

"What is it," Leslie asked.

"It was never about me. Well, not directly anyway. He led Brian and the others into a trap."

"Excuse me," Kristie exclaimed.

"I believe that he thinks that I will yield to him completely if he already controls most of my people," Rowland explained to the others.

"And you will if that's the only option. You may be the strongest and the best of us, but you are no fighter," Kristie pointed out.

"That may be somewhat true. However, the smartest members of this pack still remain free of this evil son of a bitch. Plus, we have our own way of breaking a mental control," Rowland said, not looking at any of them.

"Without Brian, how can we get into peoples' heads," Kim asked. She was biting at her nails while she paced the floor thinking.

Rowland looked up at Kim and smiled. "Who said anything about peoples' heads? I was thinking the minds of the beasts."

"That's crazy. Brian wouldn't be able to…" Kim froze in mid sentence. She realized what Rowland was getting at and didn't like it. "You are insane. I don't have that kind of power."

"What are you two talking about," Kristie wondered out load.

"Our fearless leader here thinks that I have the power to break the mages hold and bring the wolves back to our side," Kim explained. "I may be able to sway the lowest of them back, but I don't have the power to bring over the strongest."

"How do you know what limits your gifts have? We have never put your powers to the test. And, in wolf form, you power to control nature is greater."

"It may not even work in my other form," Kim said, anger helping her to keep from curling up and crying.

"We have to try," Rowland told her, grabbing her hands in his. "Focus on Brian first, but keep out of sight. If we free him, he can help with the others."

"I will try," Kim said.

"What about the rest of us," Kristie asked. Kristie's eyes had already gone amber with the thrill of the hunt so close. Sometimes Kristie scared Rowland, though he wouldn't ever let her know that.

"I want the rest of you to focus on the sirens. Keep them off me while I deal with the mage. Though, try to let them live. We don't know that they are truly evil. Once they are free from the mage, they may end up being a nice new ally," Rowland instructed. "Of course, don't get yourselves killed trying not to kill them."

"You know that we wouldn't let those hags get us before we got them," stated Sherry. "In fact, I can't wait to cut up those bitches." Sherry smiled at the look that Rowland gave her at her comment. So she added, "I said cut them, not kill them. I'm sure they are tough enough to hold up with a few flesh wounds."

"Well, we will see how well you all hold up against them. This will decide whether our combat training has paid off," Rowland told them as they began to head out of the house. For the first time he was thankful that Brian had made them do drills incase something bad ever happened.

"I'm sure we will be fine," Kristie interjected. "Brian taught us all well. And we all know that he is great in combat situations. I just hope that Kim can break the hold that I'm sure the mage has on him before we have to fight our pack brothers."

No one said anything else as they headed out the back door. The situation seemed more real now that they were out in the open. The excitement that some of the women had been feeling had disappeared; and had been replaced by worry that weighed thickly in the air around them.

Sherry and Olivia shifted into their wolf form without being instructed to do so. They knew that their beasts would have a better chance of tracking down Brian and the others. Of course, they also had shifted because they had been the ones that were most worried; and their beasts would help turn that back into excitement.

They took off in the direction that their wolf brothers had gone. No one spoke as they ventured through the dark wooded area. Even with the sun shining the woods seemed to have swallowed the darkest hours of night. The darkness didn't really affect the werewolves much, even in their human forms.

After a few minutes of moving at top speed without making a sound. Not even the leaves rustled as the wolves ran.

Rowland had a second to think that it was odd that they hadn't made a sound. Even on the hunt the leaves or twigs on the ground would give away their location. He noticed that it seemed as if mother nature herself had wanted them to find their missing companions. That's when

Rowland realized that his thoughts weren't very misplaced. He could feel the energy coming off of Kim. She didn't even seem to notice that she had calmed the woods around them. Rowland knew that her eyes would have gone past the amber color that their eyes went when they got angry and close to changing. Her eyes had gone straight to the iridescent forest green that her wolf had. Rowland thought that her green eyes in the face of her rust colored wolf was always a stunning sight to witness. Though, people said the same of his ice blue eyes set in the face of his own white wolf.

Rowland slowed to a stop as he scented feathers.

Without even being instructed to, the others stopped as well. Sherry and Olivia went to stand on either side of their Alpha, their hackles raised as in response to the danger that lay in the clearing just past the tree line they were hidden behind.

"Kim," Rowland whispered. When she turned around, showing her glowing green eyes, Rowland realized that those eyes were breathtaking in her human form as well. The green complemented the mocha color of her skin very well. "I need you to go around and flank them. That way you will most likely have a chance to free Brian without trouble. Also, could you tone your energy down a bit? You may give us away."

"Oh, sorry Rowland," Kim said, blushing in the dark. "I hadn't realized I was doing anything. Hell, I didn't know I had this power in human form."

"Well," Kristie added. "Looks like our girl here has been holding out on us. I don't think you will even need to shift for you power boost."

"Kristie," Rowland hissed at her. "Knock it off. You don't have to be mean to Kim right now; we have a crisis to fix before you have to worry about having your position in the pack challenged." "I'm not worried that she could take me," Kristie spat with disgust in her tone. Kristie never thought that Kim was good enough, or dominant enough, to be the packs 4th in command. Kim's gentle nature had always been a sign of weakness to some of the others. Yet, she took down her challengers with grace and tenderness that shouldn't have been possible, especially for a werewolf. Now, when danger was eminent; her powers true potential was showing. And Kristie wasn't happy with that.

A moment later, they heard foot steps coming up behind them. It sounded like two human men.

'Who would be out here this late?' Rowland was starting to wonder if the mage had gathered human followers to aid them. And, if he had, would he be willing to take them out before they could give away their position.

After what seemed like an hour, which was really only five minutes, they could hear voices that went with the footfalls.

"Shit," Rowland said under his breath as he realized who the voices belonged to. "I guess they must have been watching the house after what happened with Rudi."

"Jeff and Darvis," Kristie asked.

"Yes," Rowland said. He didn't feel the need to elaborate the extent of danger Jeff and Darvis were walking into. Rowland knew that they were upset and probably wouldn't listen to him when he tells them to turn back. Though, he had to try.

Rowland turned in the direction of the voices and bolted toward them. He didn't even tell the others what he was doing. He just left them standing in the small area that was thick with trees and bushes. He knew that they would be safe, not only because they were out of sight; but because they could definitely handle themselves. The women in his pack were just as strong as the males; sometimes more so.

It only took Rowland a few seconds to track down the officers that were following them. Their navy blue uniforms standing out easily in the mid-afternoon sun as they passed gaps in the canopy. Both Jeff and Darvis had their guns un-holstered and at their sides while they ran. Rowland didn't like how tense they both were as he stepped out into the path in front of them.

"Freeze," Jeff ordered. He and Darvis had their guns raised and aimed at Rowland without thinking about it.

"You really don't want me to do that," Rowland told them with a smirk spreading across his face. He knew they meant stop; but having ice vision at his disposal could put a swing on the old phrase.

"Rowland," Jeff said, clearly relieved that it wasn't someone or something else in front of him. He and Darvis lowered their weapons and walked over to the werewolf standing in their way. "We could have shot you. Are you *still* barking mad?"

"No. However, you two need to get out of here. This area is about to become very dangerous for humans to be present," Rowland told them, dropping his friendly joking attitude that he usually used with the local police.

"We can't do that," Darvis said. Darvis' face showed lines that Rowland had never seen on the man before. Clearly anger was not a good look for him. "We have an officer in the I.C.U. We have to catch the guy responsible."

"Well, I'm right here," Rowland said. He too was starting to get angry; and having an angry werewolf with his kinda powers was not something that an cop could handle. Even with silver at their disposal, he could rip them to shreds before they could cause his serious injury.

"What do you mean by that," Jeff said. He was the only one that seemed to be able to keep his cool.

"What I mean is that my plan had repercussions," Rowland growled at him. He wasn't angry at the officers for looking for the guy responsible for putting Rudi in the hospital. He was pissed at himself for not being able to control himself when he was taken over. "I let the mage take control and he used me to attack my wolves. Rudi, being new, didn't stand a chance."

"Rowland," Darvis said. He seemed torn between being angry at the big wolf and being sympathetic toward him. "Let us help you."

"I can't do that," Rowland told them. "I wish I could, but I can't put you in danger. He has control of half my pack already. We have a plan. I have my cell with me. Just stay here and I will call you when we bring them down. Then, you can arrest anyone left alive."

"Sure thing," Jeff piped out before Darvis could argue anymore.

"Your right," Darvis agreed after a few seconds. "After my run in with one demon, I think I can let you guys handle this shit. Good luck."

"Thanks." And, without another word, Rowland turned and rushed back to his remaining pack.

17: Disappear

owland caught up with his wolves moments later. All of them seemed to be on pins and needles in anticipation for the battle that was only moments in their future.

"Are you girls ready," Rowland asked as a rhetorical question.

Kim turned toward him and nodded; and, without a word, disappeared into the dense woods.

The others formed a line as they prepared to advance into the little clearing that was just on the other side of the stretch of woods that concealed them from their enemies. Kristie was out in front, ready to lead her sisters into battle. While Rowland veered off in the opposite direction of Kim.

He had instructed Kristie to begin their advance as soon as he was out of sight. He was going to try and flank the mage, if he could. His hope was that he could take him out without a fight.

Rowland poked his head through the branches and bushes enough to catch a glimpse of the clearing. What he found was the other half of his pack, all in wolf form, resting in a circle around a young man. The young man appeared to be around fifteen or so. His eyes were closed in what looked like a meditative state. He had sandy blonde with pale complexion. His clothing wouldn't have been out of place at any school. No one would ever suspect that this young man could have been the cause to all of this trouble.

After seeing that his pack brothers weren't in human form, Rowland thought it may be best if he transformed into his wolf form himself. He ducked back into the trees to begin the quick, yet painful process of shifting. Some people may believe it to be an easy transition between human and animal forms. However, it is far from it. One's bones had to break and reform. His or her organs had to be shifted around. Muscles tore and reshaped. Though, once the shift was complete, the pain went away quickly.

In his wolf form, Rowland crouched low to the ground and crawled into the clearing. When he could see the clearing again, he saw that Brian and the other wolves in the mage's control were all awake and glaring at the other half of the pack as they emerged from the tree line. Kristie was the only one not in wolf form already. Rowland knew that she was the fastest at going through the change and would have no trouble doing so in a bind. He also knew that she was lethal in either form. Rowland wondered if she had trained in martial arts before Brian had taught them; or if she just studied really hard to impress Brian.

After a moment of staring at the wolves that were squaring off against one another, Rowland realized that the sirens were no where to be seen. So, he looked up at the trees to find nests the size of La-Z-Boys located in five different places. 'There must be more sirens than I had thought,' Rowland thought to himself . Then he realized that, from those nests, the sirens surely had seen them coming. That's when he felt someone watching him.

He looked back into the clearing to find that the mage had opened his eyes and had them boring into his own as they met. The mage had one blue and one brown eye. At first Rowland was a little freaked by the eyes.

Rowland, though keeping his eyes locked with those of the mage, was also looking for a sign of Kim at the same time. He noticed two, glowing green eyes that were almost the same color as the leaves themselves. He hoped that she worked fast because the other wolves were advancing on his remaining pack.

"So," the mage said to Rowland. "The great Alpha has come to get his pups back I see. Allow me to introduce myself. I am Donavon. As you may have figured out, I am a mage. I sensed your pack members going to the filthy succubus for information. And, I'm sure you have deduced, I am quite young. Bet you hadn't expected that."

Rowland just rolled his eyes at the young man as he ranted out an introduction. Rowland didn't care who he was or how old; he just wanted to get his pack back and make the supernatural community safe again.

"Not a talker I take it," Donavon stated. "Well, I am sure that we have time for me to explain why I am doing *what* I am doing. However, I don't think that you are really wanting to hear it. And I would hate being the cliché bad guy that reveals his plot to lure you into a trap and take over. That is just so not the evil master mind style anymore.

"Instead," Donavon continued. "I offer a deal. You, and the rest of your pack join me and I will give those that I have already taken from you back their free will."

Rowland, still staring at Donavon, just yawned and lay down. He was trying to show the mage that he was bored and that Donavon was just wasting his breath.

Before Donavon continued with an explanation of his offer, their was a whimper made by one of the other wolves. Though, with them all piled together, after starting to fight while Donavon had been trying to put Rowland to sleep, it was hard to decide which wolf was in pain.

That was until the largest one of them came stumbling out, shaking his massive his head, Rowland realized who was in pain. The wolf was almost completely black, with a white spot over each of his dark brown/green eyes and a strip of white on his chest. Rowland knew it was Brian. Although, his eyes weren't right some how.

After a moment of shaking his head and rubbing it against the ground; Brian just collapsed. Rowland started to get up and go to him when he felt Brian's familiar presence in his mind pushing against his mental defenses.

'I'm fine. Just end this before someone else gets hurt,' Brian projected. He continued to lay there and catch his breath.

Kristie, panic on her face, ran over to her fallen pack mate. "BRIAN," She screamed. She had tears running down her face by the time she reached him. Which was pretty quick, seeing how the movement from one point to the other would have appeared instantaneous to the eyes of a human.

She knelt down and held his head in her lap as she wept. Rowland couldn't even make out what she was saying over her sobs and sniffles.

Rowland could just barely see Brian's face as he winked at him just before turning and licking Kristie in the face.

In her state of panic, Kristie hit Brian across the muzzle; sending him sailing through the air to land about five feet away.

Brian hopped to his feet as soon as he landed and bounded toward Kristie again. He tackled her to the ground, pinning her, and began licking her face some more.

Rowland had to shake his head at the two of them. Not ten feet away the rest of the pack was still in disarray and here they are, goofing off. He was happy to see the two of them so happy together. It was then that he resolved that he would be changing Stephen as soon as he got a chance.

Turning back to where the mage stood; stunned that Brian was free of his control. "I don't understand," Donavon pondered. "How could he have broken free?"

Donavon finally turned his attention back to the hulking wolf that had him in his icy stare. Donavon clearly wasn't happy to see that he had lost one of his greatest weapons. He looked to the sky; and, without a word, called the sirens to the battle field.

"I know that their song wont work on you; since you aren't into girls," the mage said. "But their talons can rip you to little pieces."

Rowland realized that the mage must not have known that Kim was the one that had freed Brian from his spell. He must have thought that Rowland himself had done it. Maybe he suspected the Alpha call had freed him.

That didn't matter now because he knew that he couldn't fight off all of the sirens alone and the others were a bit preoccupied. Or at least he thought they were, until Brian and Kristie appeared at his flanks. Three on four seemed to be a bit better odds. Plus, he could hear more whimpers and knew that others would soon be free.

The sirens appeared in the sky; flying circles like many predatory birds do before they dive for their strike. Then, one by one, they began to plummet toward the earth and the wolves that were staring up at them; awaiting their gruesome fate.

Just before the sirens reached Rowland, Brian, and Kristie, there was a gun shot from behind them. One of the sirens let out a howl of pain just before a second shot went straight through her skull. She landed in a crumpled heap in front of the wolves with blood and thicker things leaking from what remained of her skull.

"Guess silver works on the winged hags as well," Darvis' stated as he and Jeff made their way into the clearing.

Jeff fired another shot, taking out another one of the winged creatures that had been diving at his friend.

The two remaining sirens, clearly not liking their odds, turned around and flew off into the afternoon sun.

"Damn it," Donavon swore. "I was trying to help you!"

Rowland, confused by the last statement, decided to shift back into his human form. Being a wolf had its perks, but it did lack in some departments. Verbal communication being one of them.

"What do you mean you were trying to help us," Rowland inquired of the mage.

"I wasn't trying to enslave you to harm people," Donavon began to explain. "I have been trying to raise an army to take on the coming darkness."

"That's fucking bullshit," Darvis said angrily, raising his gun and pointing it at the young man before them.

The mage, seeing the gun being raised at him, started chanting a spell that sent a wave of energy at Darvis, knocking the gun free of his hand as well as planting him on his ass.

Without thinking of what he was doing, Rowland turn with steam billowing from his eyes as he sent the most powerful ice beam he had ever mustard up before. This was the first time that he had ever displayed that he could use that ability while in human form before.

Just before the beam hit the mage, the mage pointed at Darvis. The mage's eyes flashed, and there was a popping noise that echoed in the open expanse of the clearing. A second later, the mage stood there like a real-to-life ice sculpture.

Rowland could see movement out of the corner of his eye as Ashlee dashed across the open space to smash into the froze form of Donavon. When he collided with the ice man, Donavon shattered into hundreds of little shards.

"Ashlee, you dumbass! We could have questioned him when he thawed about what was coming," Rowland scolded his friend.

"Sorry," Ashlee said in a sarcastic tone. "I just get tired of not being the one in control as it is. And that jackass made me a zombie that was trapped in my own mind."

"Huh," Rowland said, clearly not really that bothered by the fact that the mage was dead. After all, he had mind raped him quite often. "Who knew that you had a mind to be trapped in."

Rowland turned to thank Darvis and Jeff for their help. As he did, he witnessed Jeff kneeling where Rowland had last seen Darvis on his ass. Only, Darvis wasn't anywhere in sight. All that remained was a space of charred earth.

18: The Back of the Milk Carton

hat the hell did that crazy bastard do to him," Jeff asked as though expecting the answer to fall from the heavens. He had been a cop for many years and seen a lot of things go down; however, there normally was at least part of a body. It was almost as if Darvis had just disappear. Part of Jeff wished that were true. Though, wishing never got anyone very far on the force and Jeff knew that.

"Jeff," Rowland began, but was at a loss for words. So, he just walked over to him and placed a comforting hand on his shoulder. Rowland hadn't known Darvis long; but he had liked what he knew of the man. He could only imagine the fathoms of which Jeff's grief for his fallen comrade would reach. Being from a small town, Rowland knew that Jeff had never lost a man in the line of duty before. 'If only they had listened and stayed back, may be they would have been safe,' Rowland thought to himself; though Brian, he knew, was listening in.

'This isn't your fault,' Brian told him. 'Their job is to uphold justice and you couldn't have stopped them if you had really wanted to. Though, I read the last thought from the mage. Apparently he viewed Darvis as a threat some how. Oh, and he didn't perform a spell to cause harm to Darvis either. I'm not even sure what happened. Maybe he messed up on the mental incantation when he sensed that you were about to retaliate.'

'Are you saying that the mage may not have done this,' Rowland thought with skepticism. 'He had to have done it. No one else that was in this clearing has that kind of power. It's not like he did it to himself!'

'All I'm saying is that he hadn't meant harm,' Brian projected, while physically raising his hands to say that he had been misunderstood. 'It seemed like a transport spell. Though, he hadn't thought of a destination. Which means Darvis, if he survived the transport, could be anywhere.'

'So, this isn't murder after all,' Rowland realized. 'Fill Jeff in with the information you have. We will let him take point on this. Though, calling it a missing persons may be hard to explain. Especially when he could be anywhere. And I know for a fact that humans rarely survive being transported over very long distances.'

'I will,' Brian said, beginning to turn. He stopped mid-turn, wagging his tail, and thought, 'You may want to put your clothes back on.' He finished turning, laughing his wheezy wolf laugh as he did.

Brian went over to Jeff and began filling him in on what he had plucked from the mind of the mage just before he got blasted.

"I guess I should get forensics out here to look for any clues from this charred area," Jeff said out load. He seemed to be more focused with the prospect that Darvis may still be alive, somewhere. "If they don't find anything, we may have to bury an empty box and continue the search off the record. I'm not looking forward to talking with his wife."

Rowland had no clue how much Brian had told him as he emerged from the tree line again, where his clothes had been hidden. "That would be a good idea to have forensics come in," Rowland agreed. "Who knows? Maybe it will give us some insight to where we may be able to find Darvis."

"That was my thought exactly," Jeff admitted. "Though, I think an area filled with werewolves may be a bad idea when the other police officers arrive. I will call them up while you clear out."

"What are you going to say to them," Kristie asked, coming up behind them. "I'm sure the truth would land you in the loony bin."

"You are probably right. I'm sure keeping a few detail out wouldn't hurt. Mainly the part where a werewolf froze the culprit; and, before we could question him, another wolf smashed him. Oh, and the fact that Darvis literally vanished before our eyes. Otherwise, it will be entirely the truth." "So, you're saying that you are going to make the whole thing up," Rowland interjected. After hearing it spoken out load, Rowland realized just how crazy the truth would be.

Jeff just smiled at his old friend and turned away. As he began to walk away from the three wolves, he pulled out his phone and called the station.

Rowland knew that he and his wolves were no longer needed out here. Plus, he didn't want Jeff to have to explain to his Chief why he had so many civilians at the scene when they had been tracking a murderer. They tend to frown upon stuff like that. So, he rounded up his pack and headed back up to his house. He was dreading the clean up after he went into berserker mode while under control of Donavon.

19: Aftermath

hile they walked, Rowland kept running the mage's last words around in his head. 'What could be worse than some murdering lunatic taking control of others with his mind? He wouldn't exactly be a stable leader for one thing. Also, what could he have been afraid of? If he was scared of this coming 'darkness,' would my pack and I really fear it as well? Or, is it something that is actually good? He was evil after all; may be his views were a little obtuse.'

"You should really quit thinking so much," Brian told Rowland, having returned to human form so that no one would spot a giant wolf walking around in the woods in Illinois. "My head is killing me already. Plus, I can't turn off my telepathy after being under the control of the mage. I'm glad that my telekinesis isn't acting this strangely."

"I will try to keep my thinking to a minimum," Rowland said, putting his mental shield back into place.

"Thank you," Brian said.

"Don't mention it," Rowland stated. "Of course, if you don't gain control again, you could always room with Ashlee. I mean, he doesn't have a brain after all."

"Funny. Very funny," Brian said sarcastically, though he was laughing at the same time. "I know someone with a brain that I can be around." Brian leaned around Rowland's back to look at Kristie.

"Who says that I want you around that often," Kristie teased.

"Fine," Brian said as if hurt. "Guess you only like me in wolf form."

That made both Brian and Kristie laugh. Some one passing by them would never guess the kind of day that they had had. They may wonder why half of them were in the nude, but other than that, things would appear normal. Though, Rowland was glad that they could joke around a little at a time like this. He knew that the shock of what had just transpired hadn't hit them. He really wasn't looking forward to when it did. However, his mind was focused on one thing when he got home.

And that was making things right with Stephen. 'Guess we are going to have another wolf turning at the full moon next week. We are going to have our hands full with them.'